AND ANTHONY SHERWOOD LAUGHED

Francis Durbridge

WILLIAMS & WHITING

The script in this book was sourced from the
BBC Written Archive Centre
and the transcriptions have been made by the publisher
and have not been checked for accuracy by the BBC.

Cover design by Timo Schroeder

9781912582525

Williams & Whiting (Publishers)
15 Chestnut Grove, Hurstpierpoint,
West Sussex, BN6 9SS

Titles by Francis Durbridge published by Williams & Whiting
1   The Scarf – tv serial
2   Paul Temple and the Curzon Case – radio serial
3   La Boutique – radio serial
4   The Broken Horseshoe – tv serial
5   Three Plays for Radio Volume 1
6   Send for Paul Temple – radio serial
7   A Time of Day – tv serial
8   Death Comes to The Hibiscus – stage play
    The Essential Heart – radio play
    (writing as Nicholas Vane)
9   Send for Paul Temple – stage play
10 The Teckman Biography (tv serial)
11 Paul Temple and Steve (radio serial)
12 Twenty Minutes From Rome
13 Portrait of Alison
14 Paul Temple: Two Plays for Radio Volume 1
15 Three Plays for Radio Volume 2
16 The Other Man
17 Paul Temple and the Spencer Affair
18 Step In The Dark
19 My Friend Charles
20 A Case For Paul Temple
21 Murder In The Media
22 The Desperate People
23 Paul Temple: Two Plays for Television

Murder At The Weekend – the rediscovered newspaper serials
and short stories

Also published by Williams & Whiting:
Francis Durbridge : The Complete Guide
By Melvyn Barnes

The Doll
The Female of the Species (The Girl from the Hibiscus and
Introducing Gail Carlton)
The Man From Washington
The Passenger
The World of Tim Frazer
Tim Frazer and the Salinger Affair
Tim Frazer and the Mellin Forrest Mystery

INTRODUCTION

Francis Durbridge (1912-98) was a prolific writer of sketches, stories and plays for BBC radio from 1933. They were mostly light entertainments, including libretti for musical comedies, but a talent for crime fiction became evident in his early radio plays *Murder in the Midlands* (1934) and *Murder in the Embassy* (1937). Then in 1938 he introduced his most durable creation, the dream team of novelist/detective Paul Temple and his wife Steve.

The eight-episode radio serial *Send for Paul Temple* was an immediate success, and it led to many sequels until 1968 that secured for Durbridge an enormous UK and European fanbase. In the mid-twentieth century radio detectives were extremely popular, with Paul Temple's rivals including Dick Barton (by Edward J. Mason), Philip Odell (by Lester Powell), Dr. Morelle (by Ernest Dudley), P.C. 49 (by Alan Stranks) and Ambrose West (by Philip Levene).

Durbridge regarded himself predominantly as a playwright, even though most of his radio and television serials were novelised. As well as writing the Paul Temple serials, he contributed to BBC radio for many years with numerous productions under his own name and he also used the pseudonyms Frank Cromwell, Nicholas Vane and Lewis Middleton Harvey. And in 1952, while continuing to write for radio, he embarked on a sequence of BBC television serials (not featuring the Temples) that achieved huge viewing figures until 1980. Then from 1971 in the UK, and beginning even earlier in Germany, he wrote nine intriguing stage plays that are still produced by professional and amateur companies.

While much of the above information will already be known to Durbridge fans, the six twenty-minute radio episodes entitled *And Anthony Sherwood Laughed* will come as a revelation. Broadcast on the then BBC Forces Programme from 20 December 1940 to 31 January 1941, these short plays were produced by Martyn C. Webster – which is no surprise, as Webster had produced most of Durbridge's plays and serials since 1934 and was recognised as having "discovered" Francis Durbridge. The series was heralded in the *Radio Times* with the announcement - "This evening at 7.15 a new series by the author of the Paul Temple serials gets under way. The hero is Anthony Sherwood, gentleman and crook."

As the *Radio Times* implied, this was very different from what listeners had come to expect of Durbridge – there was no whodunit element, no master criminal to be unmasked, but simply a succession of romps with "The Prince of Rogues" turning the tables on those who deserved everything he meted out to them. There were also some nice touches of humour, including in one episode Sherwood's alibi that at the crucial time he was staying in Paul Temple's country house!

Only one actor was identified in the *Radio Times* - Stuart Vinden as Anthony Sherwood – and each week only the characters were listed. Nevertheless, during researches in the British Library and the BBC Written Archives, I identified the following actors although they could not be matched to specific roles – Janet Joye, Mabel France, Alan Robinson, Godfrey Baseley, Vincent Curran, Lester Mudditt, Hal Bryant, Marjorie Westbury and William Hughes. They might, indeed, be collectively described as the 1930s/40s Durbridge and Webster repertory company!

Although the Paul Temple serials were broadcast in various European countries from 1939, in their own languages and using their own actors, it took longer for *And Anthony Sherwood Laughed* to attract a foreign broadcaster. Indeed this appears to have been a limited attraction because the German radio version, *Bahn frei für Anthony Sherwood* (23

August 1951), translated by Friedel Schlemmer, consisted only of the first episode.

It is worth putting Sherwood in the context of Francis Durbridge's early radio career, given that his first radio credit on 25 July 1933, *The Three-Cornered Hat*, was a play for children that was far removed from the crime genre in which he was to gain international renown. He followed it with more children's stories and plays and lighthearted musical shows, then his first serious drama *Promotion* was broadcast on 3 October 1934. At that stage, within a prolific output, his crime fiction credentials began to emerge. *Murder in the Midlands* (1934) and *Murder in the Embassy* (1937) are already mentioned above as keynote productions, but the most significant demonstration of his new trend was the series of career-defining radio serials *Send for Paul Temple* (1938), *Paul Temple and the Front Page Men* (1938) and *News of Paul Temple* (1939). They established him as the master of the radio thriller serial, although he continued to write for radio in other genres.

Following *And Anthony Sherwood Laughed* (1940/41) Durbridge continued with his light-hearted scripts until he introduced another radio detective – with Carl Bernard featuring in *The Man from Washington*. In this series of six twenty-minute episodes from 23 May to 27 June 1941, Bernard featured as Johnny Cordell, an American detective assisting Scotland Yard. So it is clear that at this stage Durbridge was leaving his options open on radio, and not necessarily feeling confident that Paul Temple and Steve would survive as his main attraction on their own.

This versatility was further demonstrated by the fact that after *The Man from Washington* Durbridge adopted his pseudonym Nicholas Vane, and in rapid succession wrote six fifteen-minute plays *The Girl at the Hibiscus* (22 August to 26 September 1941) and the serial *Death Comes to the Hibiscus*

(28 November 1941 to 20 February 1942). Then, using another pseudonym Lewis Middleton Harvey, he wrote the eight-episode radio serial *Mr Hartington Died Tomorrow* (9 February to 6 April 1942), which proved to be a winner as new productions were broadcast later in 1942 and in 1950.

So we have no radio recording of *And Anthony Sherwood Laughed* and no novel, but we can now celebrate the fact that these original scripts have been unearthed and finally published after over eighty years.

Melvyn Barnes
Author of *Francis Durbridge: The Complete Guide* (Williams & Whiting, 2018)

This book reproduces Francis Durbridge's original script together with the list of characters and actors of the BBC programme on the dates mentioned, but the eventual broadcast might have edited Durbridge's script in respect of scenes, dialogue and character names.

AND
ANTHONY SHERWOOD
LAUGHED

A series of six episodes
By FRANCIS DURBRIDGE
Broadcast on BBC Radio
20 December 1940 – 31 January 1941

Episode One

Make Way For Anthony Sherwood

CHARACTERS:

ANTHONY SHERWOOD

MRS DIMBLE (NANNY)

CHIEF INSPECTOR HUDSON

CEDAR

BENNY LAWRENCE

JANICE WILSON

ERIC RAYNOR

SERGEANT RAWLINGS

AN EDITOR

MR GRANT

KAREN

DOBSON

A WAITRESS

Introductory music … Opening announcement …
FADE music

… CROSS FADE with the sound of an approaching car. The car stops … The engine is still running …
There is a pause.
CEDAR is the first to speak. He is a rather dreamy Irishman …

CEDAR: So you've never been to God's country, eh Benny? You've never had the smell o' the Bronx in your nostrils an' seen Manhattan lights playing the very devil over the East river …

BENNY: (*Nervously*) Cedar … what time is it?

CEDAR: (*As if coming out of a dream*) Time? Time … did you say? Time … Benny, me boy … is but an infinitesimal fragment snatched from the very …

BENNY: Cedar … for God's sake!

There is a slight pause.

CEDAR: (*Softly*) It's nine minutes past ten, he should be here any minute … Nervous?

BENNY: (*Far too sure of himself to be convincing*) … What me? Not on your sweet life …

CEDAR: (*Scornfully, laughing*) … Ah! You're as nervous as hell, Benny.

BENNY: All right! All right! I'm nervous! So what?

CEDAR: So just this … me bonny blue-eyed boy. No slip-ups. No getting the wind in your sails before the devil arrives.

BENNY: Don't worry, I'm not that nervous. We'll get Sherwood all right … this time.

CEDAR: We've got to get him, Benny!

A car is heard. It is approaching at a tremendous speed.

3

BENNY: Here he is ... Get those lights out ... Now get down ...

CEDAR: Put the gun on the side or ... Steady! Steady, my boy.

The car draws level. There is a sudden splutter of a machine-gun and the smashing of glass. The car skids, and in order to correct itself, gathers speed ...

BENNY: (*Angry*) Blast! The car skidded ...

CEDAR: (*Wildly; furious*) You've missed him! You've missed him, Benny.

FADE IN music.

CROSS FADE with telephone ringing.

FADE bell ...

EDITOR: ... That you, Morgan? Listen, there's been another attempt on Anthony Sherwood. No, they missed him. Damn near squeak though. What? I'll say somebody's after him ... a guy doesn't have three phoney accidents in a week ... not in this town. (*Exasperated*) Yes. Yes, I know Sherwood won't talk ... but surely somebody will!! Now listen, Morgan, I'm only the editor of this classic journal but ... (*Fade*) ...

FADE IN music.

FADE DOWN.

MR GRANT: (*A gentle, educated voice*) Anthony Sherwood? Oh, yes ... He was here for quite a time. I do believe he was Captain of House for about two terms ... or was it three? ...I just forget ... M'm? ... No, I can't say I really liked him ... always gave one the impression he treated life rather as a sort of ... er ...

4

flippant gesture ... Oh, no ... Not what one would call a studious boy ... (*Suddenly emphatically*) Oh yes ... Charming! Quite charming!!

FADE IN music.

FADE DOWN.

KAREN: (*A warm, gentle voice*) I only met Tony Sherwood once. It was on a P and O liner leaving Honolulu. The day we met I lost a ring ... a sapphire ring ... it was very valuable (*with a sigh*) ... But he was sweet ... very, very sweet ...

FADE IN music.

FADE DOWN

DOBSON: (*A crisp military voice*) Well, as a matter of fact Sherwood was articled to the firm ... 1912 I think it was ... just before the war. Seemed a damned decent chap I thought. Don't think he'd have made much of a lawyer but ... M'm ... Oh, no ... he left. Some sort of a stink about five hundred quid. Funny sort of business, altogether. Didn't seem to worry Sherwood very much ... So far as I can remember ... he ... er ... just laughed.

FADE IN music.

Slow FADE.

CROSS FADE with Anthony Sherwood laughing. It is gay, yet somewhat roguish, laughter.

SHERWOOD: My dear Nanny, you can hardly expect me to spend the rest of my life in the flat, just

5

because some gentlemen of rather doubtful ancestry decide to take a pot at me.

NANNY: But it's the third time it's happened in a week. Oh. I do wish you'd take care of yourself, Tony.

MRS DIMBLE, commonly called 'NANNY' is ANTHONY SHERWOOD's housekeeper. She is a homely though occasionally quick tempered, widow of about sixty.

SHERWOOD: But I do take care of myself! And tonight I shall take extra care, I assure you. (*Magnanimously*) I shall start with a bottle of Paul Aget 24 … (*Correcting himself*) … or rather <u>we</u> shall start with a bottle of …

NANNY: We? Oh, so it's like that it is, my boy!

SHERWOOD: What do you mean "it's like that"? Mrs Dimble, every now and again, a wealth of meaning seems to creep into your voice which, to say the least, indicates a somewhat ribald imagination.

NANNY: Well, if you must know, I was thinking of Clare Denson … (*Under her breath*) … fast hussy!

SHERWOOD: Now that's where you're mistaken, Mrs Dimble. Beneath that brittle make-up of Clare's there beats a heart of gold … or platinum, of course one can't be too certain.

NANNY: Yes, well I don't like her, and I don't care who knows it!

SHERWOOD: I'm sure you don't, Nanny.

NANNY: (*Still rather upset*) And besides I'm … I'm worried, Tony.

SHERWOOD: Of course you are! (*Affectionately*) It's all right, Nanny, I've got my wits about me, now don't you worry.

6

NANNY:	Yes, but … it's never been like this before. First the car smash … then that awful business with the poison … and then the machine gun. There's been accidents an' things I know, but this is different … it's so … callous … so deliberate …
SHERWOOD:	(*Reflectively*) Yes, so deliberate. Which makes me think it must be our old friend Raynor.
NANNY:	(*Surprised*) But why should it be Raynor?
SHERWOOD:	Well, after all, I did relieve him of the best part of seventeen thousand.
NANNY:	Yes, but that was a long time ago!
SHERWOOD:	Eric Raynor has an excellent memory; he assured me on that point at the time.
NANNY:	In any case you only used six thousand for … er …
SHERWOOD:	Personal expenses …
NANNY:	… the rest went to charity.
SHERWOOD:	M'm – I don't think Eric Raynor exactly approves of charity, Nanny, at least not if it's very far afield.
NANNY:	(*Thoughtfully*) Of course, it might be Hollis. I supposed you'd thought of that?
SHERWOOD:	Yes. Yes … it might be Lou Hollis. That was six thousand, wasn't it?
NANNY:	Eight. And pretty well all for …
SHERWOOD:	… charity …
NANNY:	M'm – very personal too, if you ask me! That was the time you were friendly with Diane Sloane.
SHERWOOD:	Ah … Diane! A girl in a thousand!
NANNY:	A girl in eight thousand might be a little more appropriate!

7

The telephone commences to ring,

SHERWOOD: (*Amused*) Perhaps you're right. (*He lifts the receiver*) Hello? … Yes … Anthony Sherwood speaking! … Who? … (*Suddenly, very pleasant*) Why hello Inspector! Where are you speaking from … (*Surprised*) But of course, Inspector! … My dear Hudson, don't be silly … Delighted to see you … Yes, straight away … Of course, my dear fellow … Of course! (*Replaces receiver*)

NANNY: (*Apprehensively*) Tony, that wasn't …?

SHERWOOD: Chief-Inspector George St. John Hudson.

NANNY: He's – not coming here?

SHERWOOD: Yes, I'm afraid he is. As a matter of fact he's downstairs at the moment. (*Suddenly*) What's the matter, Nanny, I thought you liked old George?

NANNY: (*Apprehensively*) Tony, why is he coming here? You haven't …

SHERWOOD: No, my dear Mrs Dimble, I haven't. I told you four years ago, that I'd finished with … er … all that sort of thing … and I meant it.

NANNY: Yes, but if that's the case why does the Inspector want to see you?

SHERWOOD: It's quite obvious why he wants to see me. The Yard are in a devil of a state about this Thursday night business. The Chief Commissioner even wanted to provide me with police protection. (*He chuckles*)

NANNY: And you refused…?

SHERWOOD: But of course …

NANNY: Oh, Tony … why?

SHERWOOD: Because I'm more than capable of looking after myself, Nanny … that's why.

8

The flat bell rings.

SHERWOOD: Here's Hudson … Leave us alone, there's a dear.

The outer door opens. CHIEF INSPECTOR HUDSON arrives. He is fairly well educated, and slightly pompous.

HUDSON: Hello, Tony! All dressed up in the glad rags, eh? Sorry to barge in like this, but the fact of the matter …

SHERWOOD: Don't be silly! Nice to see you again. Any true and trusted servant of the Yard is always welcome at the Sherwood domain, you know that, Inspector.

HUDSON: M'm.

SHERWOOD: Glass of sherry?

HUDSON: Er … no – er – not just at the moment.

SHERWOOD: Whiskey and soda?

HUDSON: Er … rather not … just now … thanks all the same.

SHERWOOD: M'm – well … you don't mind it I do?

HUDSON: No, of course not.

SHERWOOD mixes his drink.

SHERWOOD: Happy days, Inspector … and enchanting nights! (*He drinks*)

HUDSON: Next time … I should make it 'Lucky days', Tony … if I were you.

SHERWOOD: What do you mean?

Slight pause.

HUDSON: (*Quietly: rather grim*) They're after you, Tony … and this time unless I'm very much mistaken, they're going to get you!

SHERWOOD: Well, they've had three shots this week, and they were not exactly amateur performances, Inspector … but I'm still here. So you see,

9

perhaps after all, you might be .,. very much mistaken.

HUDSON: Tony, listen to me, for twelve solid years you gave Scotland Yard, and the Federal Bureau of Investigation at Washington, what one can only aptly describe as "the run around". There wasn't a wealthy man here or in the States that you didn't trim at some time or another. You blazed a trail from London to Vienna and from Charleston to San Francisco. Admittedly, pretty well everybody you 'rooked' was, well to say the least, of a somewhat dubious character. And since I've personally always treated you as a friend I don't mind admitting that, more often than not, you gave us boys at the Yard 'one hell of a big laugh'. But there's one little point which you seem to have overlooked, Tony, and this week certainly must have brought it home to you ... People like Lou Hollis, Eric Raynor, Rickie Shaw and Gabriel Bond ... don't forget. They're going to get you, Tony ... They're going to get you if it takes twenty years.

There is a slight pause. Anthony Sherwood starts laughing.

SHERWOOD: My dear Inspector, you sound just like Mrs Dimble! I can take care of myself, I assure you.

HUDSON: M'm – Well, I must be off ... (*Suddenly*) Oh, and by the way ... when I was coming here tonight, a thought struck me. And don't laugh, because it's not so damned funny as it sounds! I've got a hunch that having failed to

10

get rid of you one way, they may try another …

SHERWOOD: That's interesting …

HUDSON: They may try and 'frame' you, Tony … Get you a stretch for something you haven't done. Raynor, for instance, is pretty cute on turning the tables.

SHERWOOD: Is he?

HUDSON: Be mighty awkward if I had to pinch you after all these years, eh, Tony? Especially if you happened to be innocent.

SHERWOOD: But I was always innocent, Inspector, you know that. (*Slight pause*) By the way, forgive my curiosity, but who were the two gentlemen on Thursday?

HUDSON: I don't think you'd know them. A man called Cedar and a little chap named Benny Lawrence. From all accounts they were going to get pretty well paid for the job … by whom, we don't know. They're not squealers, either of them.

SHERWOOD: You suspect Raynor…?

HUDSON: Yes, but that's just my personal opinion. The Assistant Commissioner seems to think that it might be Bond.

SHERWOOD: Bond? (*Thoughtfully*) No, somehow I'm inclined to agree with your theory. Raynor always had a somewhat vicious streak.

HUDSON: Yes, but don't forget you relieved the gentleman of seventeen thousand … That didn't exactly delight him, you know. Still, I'd like to get my hands on the rat.

SHERWOOD: Would you, Inspector?

11

HUDSON: Ah, well – if things get too hot, and you change your mind about the bodyguard, give me a ring!

SHERWOOD: I'll think about it.

The flat bell rings.

HUDSON: Hello, who's this … the lady friend?

SHERWOOD: (*Slightly puzzled*) I very much doubt it.

The door opens.

JANICE: Mr Sherwood … Anthony Sherwood?

JANICE WILSON is apparently a nervous and somewhat emotional person.

SHERWOOD: Yes.

JANICE: My name is Wilson … Janice Wilson. I believe you met my brother several years ago, and I was wondering …

SHERWOOD: Oh, do come in, Miss Wilson … I'll be with you in just a second.

HUDSON: Don't bother about me, Tony, I've found my way out of better places than this.

SHERWOOD: (*Amused*) I'll give you a ring next week … we might have lunch together.

HUDSON: Why not …? I'm broad-minded.

The door closes.

SHERWOOD: Do sit down, Miss Wilson. (*Tiny pause*) Cigarette?

JANICE: (*Nervously*) No. No, thank you.

SHERWOOD: You say that I met your brother …?

JANICE: Yes … Alex.

SHERWOOD: Alex … Alex Wilson? Yes, I seem to remember the name … although the circumstances of our meeting are not so clear in my mind. Was he attached to the American Consul at Penang, by any chance?

JANICE: Yes, but only for a short time. Actually, I believe that he first met you at Vancouver. I think you were staying with Lord McLeod, and Alex came over once or twice to see you.

SHERWOOD: Yes. Yes, of course. A tall boy with slightly reddish hair.

JANICE: Auburn.

SHERWOOD: (*Slowly*) Alex Wilson …? I'm rather surprised that he remembers me. We didn't see a great deal of one another you know.

JANICE: No. I rather gather that you were never … what one might call friends. Nevertheless, he was and still is for that matter, quite an admirer of yours.

SHERWOOD: An admirer? That's rather flattering! Which particular trait in my character exactly does he find worthy of … er, admiration?

JANICE: I don't think it's quite a trait in your character that he admires, Mr Sherwood, so much as a particular incident in your … er … career.

SHERWOOD: Incident?

JANICE: Yes. You see, my brother knew Eric Raynor. He knew what an utter scoundrel he was, and when you …

SHERWOOD: Shall we say … put one over on him?

JANICE: He was naturally delighted.

SHERWOOD: I see. (*Quietly*) Miss Wilson … why did you come to see me? Is your brother in trouble?

JANICE: Yes … Yes, in terrible trouble … I'm afraid.

SHERWOOD: What exactly?

JANICE: Alex fell in love … or rather thought he was in love … with Roma Seaton. (*Angry*) Oh, the stupid idiotic boy! There are times when I simply haven't the patience to …

13

SHERWOOD: Miss Wilson, you must forgive me if I appear a little dense but …

JANICE: Oh, I'm sorry. But I'm so frightfully bad at explaining things … and all this has worried me so much that I simply don't know which way to turn.

SHERWOOD: Supposing we start at the beginning. Alex fell in love … or was infatuated shall we say? … by Roma Seaton. I presume you mean Roma Seaton … the actress?

JANICE: Yes. He was so crazy about her that he spent every single penny he had; and then to make matters worse the stupid boy borrowed seven thousand pounds with which to buy a necklace. I think he was afraid that Roma was tiring of him, and he wanted to make some sort of a final gesture.

SHERWOOD: He certainly seems to have made it if he paid seven thousand for a necklace.

JANICE: It was a lovely thing. I'm not very keen on diamonds myself, but …

SHERWOOD: Miss Seaton … accepted the necklace?

JANICE: But of course! That was about a fortnight ago, and since then she's only seen Alex once … and that was at a party.

SHERWOOD: He certainly seems to have had a raw deal.

JANICE: (*Hesitatingly*) Mr Sherwood … I said that Alex borrowed the money for the necklace, well … I'm afraid he didn't. You see, he's always been rather clever and designing and …

SHERWOOD: (*Quietly*) He forged a cheque …?

JANICE: Yes. Yes, I'm afraid so.

SHERWOOD: What's happened?

14

JANICE: He's got about a week. If he can get the cheque covered by next Thursday then …

SHERWOOD: And can he …?

JANICE: I'm afraid there's only one chance … the necklace.

SHERWOOD: (*Quietly*) Is that why you came here … to see me?

JANICE: Yes.

SHERWOOD: Wouldn't it have been better if you'd seen Miss Seaton instead?

JANICE: Roma Seaton won't return the necklace. She won't even admit that Alex gave it to her.

SHERWOOD: Of course she's under no obligation to return it … you realise that?

JANICE: (*Desperately*) Yes … Yes of course … but it's our only chance. If we can't cover the cheque then there's nothing for it but …

SHERWOOD: Does your brother know that you've come to see me about this matter?

JANICE: No; although Alex mentioned your name last night. He was terribly worried and thought perhaps you might be able to help.

SHERWOOD: I see.

A pause.

JANICE: I'm sorry, I shouldn't have come here. Naturally I ought to have realised that …

SHERWOOD: Miss Wilson, I want you to meet me at Warner's tea shop in Curzon Street … tomorrow, about four o'clock. Is that all right?

JANICE: (*Anxiously*) Does that mean that you'll get the necklace and …

SHERWOOD: It means that I want you to meet me at Warner's tea shop in Curzon Street … tomorrow, about four o'clock.

JANICE: I see. (*Suddenly*) If you do this for me, I shall never forget it … honestly I shan't. I don't want to make myself a nuisance, Mr Sherwood, but …

SHERWOOD: That's all right. (*He leads JANICE towards the door*) Now just go home and take things easy … and not a word to your brother about this, you understand?

JANICE: Yes … Yes, of course. Of course.

Door opens and closes.

Pause.

The second door opens.

SHERWOOD: Ah, Nanny! Where's the telephone directory?

NANNY: Under the telephone o' course. (*Tiny pause*) Tony, what did that girl want …?

SHERWOOD: (*Thoughtfully; studying the directory*) Which girl …? Oh! Nothing … she was rather upset about something … that's all.

NANNY: Is she a friend of yours?

SHERWOOD: (*His thoughts elsewhere*) No. I met her brother a long time ago, and she thought perhaps I might be able to help him … (*Suddenly*) Ah, here we are … Seaton … Roma Seaton, 24B, Christie Mansions, Mayfair …

NANNY: Is he in trouble …?

SHERWOOD: M'm? Oh, yes … yes, he's in trouble, Nanny. (*Reading*) Mayfair 7877 … (*He dials*) Slip into the study and get my driving licence, it's on the desk … there's a dear!

16

NANNY: (*Leaving*) I hope you're not going to be late tonight, Tony.

Door closes.

SHERWOOD: (*On the phone*) Hello … Could I speak to Miss Seaton, please? Anthony Sherwood speaking … Thank you. (*Pause*) Hello … Miss Seaton? Anthony Sherwood here … We met about four months ago at Lady Crossway's … do you remember? … Yes, that's right … Tall, dark and handsome. I also have a mole on the right knee-cap, but I don't think we got that far … (*Amused*) Of course … I intended to ring you weeks ago but I've been abroad … Oh, here and there … Not very good … actually. Really? (*Slight pause*) Well, Roma listen … couldn't we have dinner together … yes, tonight … M'm? … Supper? … Better still … I'll pick you up after the theatre … Splendid! … Yes, of course! By all means … What's that? … My dear, you must be thrilled … About eleven … Goodbye.

Replace the receiver.

The door opens.

NANNY: I've had a terrible time finding that driving licence. I thought you said …

SHERWOOD: I wonder if you'd ring up Clare for me … I can't possibly see her tonight. I'll ring her tomorrow about ten.

NANNY: Aren't you going out tonight?

SHERWOOD: Yes … only later.

NANNY: (*Apprehensively*) Tony … you've got that look in your eyes … The look you had the night you saw Raynor … The look you had the night Rickie Shaw lost …

17

SHERWOOD: (*Amused*) Have I ... Mrs Dimble?
NANNY: Tony ... is everything all right?
SHERWOOD: Absolutely, Nanny! Absolutely!
FADE IN music.

FADE DOWN.
Slow fade in of CHIEF-INSPECTOR HUDSON snoring. He is a heavy sleeper. The telephone by the side of his bed commences to ring. It is quite a little while before the INSPECTOR decides to answer it. He is still very sleepy ...

HUDSON: Hello? ... Yes ... Yes ... Hudson speaking ... Yes ... Who is it? (*Irritated*) I said ... who is it speaking? ... I've already said it's Hudson ... Surely to goodness you ... (*Suddenly*) Oh, it's you, Dixon! What is it? (*Seriously*) When? ... Roma Seaton ... That's the actress, isn't it? ... How much was the necklace worth? ... Phew! ... Yes, I'm listening ... (*Pause*) ... Yes ... When did she first realise that it ... M'm ...? ... Oh! ... Where did she go, do you know? ... Savoy ... Alone? (*Tiny pause*) I see ... Who was the boyfriend, did you find out? ... (*Staggered*) What!!! ... Sherwood ... Anthony Sherwood? ... Listen, Dixon ... are you sure? ... Holy Mackerel!!! (*Excitedly*) That's all right, Dixon ... I'll take care of this little lot ... No, don't bother, I'll have a word with the A.C. ...Yes, righto ... (*Replaces receiver*) (*Thoughtfully*) Anthony Sherwood ... Up to your old tricks, eh Tony? ... my boy? Up to your old tricks ...

FADE IN music.

18

SLOW FADE. CROSS FADE with typical restaurant orchestra playing a 'tea-time' selection. The orchestra stops.

WAITRESS: Can I get you anything else, sir?

SHERWOOD: No. No, not just at the moment thank you.

WAITRESS: Will your friend have Indian tea or China, sir?

SHERWOOD: Er … China please.

WAITRESS: Thank you.

JANICE WILSON arrives. She is excited and rather breathless.

JANICE: I'm sorry I'm late. I missed a bus at the Tottenham Court Road and that rather …

SHERWOOD: That's all right. Sit down.

JANICE: (*Excited*) I've seen the papers! You've … got the necklace?

SHERWOOD: Sh! Not so loud, please!

JANICE: Oh, I'm sorry.

SHERWOOD: What you need is tea … and plenty of it. You've got the jitters, young lady.

JANICE: I've been so frightfully nervous, I haven't really known which way to turn … When I saw the papers this morning … I felt so terribly grateful I … I didn't know what to do. I tried to get you on the phone but a Mrs Simble or Rimble said …

SHERWOOD: Dimble …

JANICE: That you were out. Then I realised how very stupid I was getting so … het up about things and I … pulled myself together.

SHERWOOD: (*Amused*) Did you? Well, I'm glad to hear that. Ah, here's the tea!

WAITRESS: Would you like anything else, miss, or …

JANICE: No, thank you. (*She pours out her cup of tea*) Oh, I see you've got yours.

19

SHERWOOD: Yes. By the way, I ordered you China tea ... I hope that's all right?

JANICE: Yes ... Yes, lovely. (*She drinks*)

A pause.

SHERWOOD: Better?

JANICE: Much. (*Suddenly*) Mr Sherwood ... have you got the necklace? I don't want to rush things, but Alex is so frightfully ...

SHERWOOD: Miss Wilson, listen ... What chance do you think your brother would have of getting rid of the necklace? Don't you realise that the whole of Scotland Yard ...

JANICE: (*Alarmed*) You ... didn't get it! You didn't ... get ... the necklace? The papers are lying ...

SHERWOOD: Miss Wilson, please ... pull yourself together! The papers aren't lying. I got the necklace all right but I wasn't such a damn fool as to stick to it. (*Softly, urgently*) Now listen – and listen carefully. Outside in the entrance hall you'll see a dark brown overcoat. It's hanging on a peg on the far side of the sweet counter. On top of the overcoat you'll see a small valise ... Now, when you leave here stroll over to the coat and take the case, and for heaven's sake, take care of it because ...

JANICE: The necklace!

SHERWOOD: No, I'm afraid it doesn't contain the necklace, Miss Wilson ... but it does contain the next best thing. The amount paid by a certain Mr Joseph Coogan for the privilege of purchasing the necklace. To be exact: four thousand pounds. Not a really

20

	good price I'm afraid, but the necklace was hot and I couldn't afford to take any chances.
JANICE:	Mr Sherwood, I'm so grateful that I haven't the remotest idea of how to thank you … I'm sure Alex will never …
SHERWOOD:	I don't want to rush you, but there's rather a lot of money in that valise and I'm not very keen on leaving it in the vestibule any longer than is absolutely necessary.

The orchestra commences to play.

JANICE:	Of course. I'll get Alex to ring you tomorrow…
SHERWOOD:	Better make it towards the end of the week. I shall be out of Town for a day or so.
JANICE:	Yes, well … goodbye, Mr Sherwood … and thanks for everything.
SHERWOOD:	Goodbye.

FADE IN orchestra.

FADE DOWN orchestra and café noises.

A door opens.

FADE IN traffic noises.

A large American sedan draws up to the kerb.

The door of the car opens.

RAYNOR:	(*Excitedly*) What happened?
JANICE:	We haven't much time, let's get going!
RAYNOR:	Is he still in the tea shop?
JANICE:	Yes.
RAYNOR:	You got the necklace?
JANICE:	No.
RAYNOR:	What!!
JANICE:	It's all right, Eric, there's nothing to get excited about.

RAYNOR:	My God, if there's been any slip-ups over this …
JANICE:	There hasn't.
RAYNOR:	But the necklace …?
JANICE:	(*Amused*) The poor dear was touched by my sentimental story about brother Alex, that he actually 'fenced' it into the bargain.
RAYNOR:	(*Staggered*) You mean he got rid of it, and simply handed over the money?
JANICE:	(*Chuckling*) Four thousand … The necklace worried him. He said it was 'hot'.
RAYNOR:	I'll say it was 'hot'! Well, that's four thousand back from that swine anyway – and with a bit of luck he should get seven years for pulling this job.
JANICE:	(*Softly*) Seven years …
RAYNOR:	Well, he's had it coming to him for a long time. Let that be a lesson to you, sweetie. There isn't a guy living who can put one over on Eric Raynor and get away with it … Not even Anthony Sherwood!!

FADE car.
FADE IN music.

FADE DOWN music.
FADE IN CHIEF INSPECTOR HUDSON speaking. He is extremely bad tempered.

HUDSON:	… My dear Mrs Dimble, I am simply asking you a perfectly straightforward question!
NANNY:	(*Exasperated*) And I am giving you a perfectly straightforward answer!
HUDSON:	Tt! But you must have seen Mr Sherwood! Surely he didn't simply walk out of the house and …

NANNY:	If I've told you once, I've told you a hundred times! Tony left the flat about two hours after you left.
HUDSON:	On Tuesday night?
NANNY:	On Tuesday night.
HUDSON:	And you haven't seen him since?
NANNY:	No.
NANNY:	And he hasn't telephoned?
NANNY:	He hasn't telephoned!
HUDSON:	(*Utterly exhausted*) Well, God knows what's happened to him! I've got every officer in London on the ... (*The telephone rings*) Hello? ... No, sir, I'm afraid we haven't. I've got Sherwood's housekeeper here but she either knows nothing or she won't talk. (*Irritated*) Well, we're doing our best, sir ... Yes ... Yes ... We've searched every hotel for miles. If Sherwood's in London we'll find him! ... I know it's urgent, but we're doing everything we can! (*Tiny pause*) Well, what do you suggest, sir? It's Anthony Sherwood we're dealing with you know! ... Yes ... Yes ... Don't worry. I'll find him all right ... Yes, sir ... Very good, sir. (*Politely*) Well, it is rather worrying you know, sir ... Very good ... (*He rings off*) Good God, the man must be crazy!
NANNY:	There seems to be a lot of crazy people in this building if you ask me.
HUDSON:	No one's asking you!
The door opens.	
HUDSON:	Well, what is it, Sergeant?
SERGEANT:	A gentleman to see you, sir.

23

HUDSON:	Damn it man, use your common sense! I'm up to my eyes in work and you barge in here as if … as if Anthony Sherwood had dropped in.
SERGEANT:	It is Anthony Sherwood, sir.
HUDSON:	Now leave me alone, Sergeant, and have the brains to realise … (*Suddenly*) It's what!!
SERGEANT:	Anthony Sherwood, sir.
HUDSON:	But – but who brought him?
SERGEANT:	He appears to have brought himself, sir.
HUDSON:	Brought … himself?
SERGEANT:	Yes, sir. He simply drove up to the main entrance and asked to see Twinkly Toes. Sergeant Thomas rather gathered that he meant you, sir.
HUDSON:	(*Controlling himself with difficulty*) Er … send him in, Sergeant … and take Mrs Dimble down to the general office.
NANNY:	I want to see Tony!
HUDSON:	You shall see Mr Sherwood the moment I've finished with him, I promise you.
NANNY:	It's to be hoped I do my boy, for your sake!

The door opens.

Pause.

The second door opens.

SHERWOOD:	Ah, hello, Inspector …
HUDSON:	Tony … where the devil have you been? I've been turning this town upside down!
SHERWOOD:	I went to the films.
HUDSON:	The films! Not for three whole days!
SHERWOOD:	It was "Gone with the Wind".
HUDSON:	(*Exasperated*) Now listen, Tony, you can laugh and you can joke but this is serious …

	damn serious. I've got a warrant out for your arrest, and this time …
SHERWOOD:	(*Gaily*) This time will be the one exception. It always is the one exception, isn't it, Inspector? Well, without wishing to be too inquisitive what precisely is the charge?
HUDSON:	The charge …? You know full well what the charge is. You took the necklace … The … Seaton Necklace.
SHERWOOD:	The Seaton necklace? (*Politely*) Has it been stolen? That's funny, I had dinner with Roma Seaton on Tuesday and she never mentioned it.
HUDSON:	(*Exasperated*) Tony … Tony … for heaven's sake!!

The telephone commences to ring.

SHERWOOD:	Ah, the telephone. How very appropriate!
HUDSON:	(*Suddenly suspicious*) What do you mean?
SHERWOOD:	Answer it, Inspector … Answer it!

Tiny pause … HUDSON lifts the receiver.

HUDSON:	Hello? … Yes, Inspector Hudson speaking … Oh, Miss Seaton!! (*To SHERWOOD*) It's Roma Seaton …
SHERWOOD:	(*Amused*) Roma Seaton! Why, I'm surprised, Inspector … you of all people!
HUDSON:	Don't be a … (*On the phone*) Yes, I'm listening … (*Quietly bewildered*) You've … what? … Yes … Yes … But surely, Miss Seaton, you must have looked there in the first place … M'm? … No, I'll have a word with the Commissioner … No, that's quite all right … I assure you it's not necessary … Yes … Yes, very well. (*Replaces*

25

	receiver ... completely nonplussed) Well ... I'm damned!
SHERWOOD:	What's happened, George, has she turned you down?
HUDSON:	(*Rather confused*) ... She's found the necklace ... apparently it was never stolen ... (*Suddenly*) I'm just beginning to see daylight ...
SHERWOOD:	How do you like it?
HUDSON:	(*Excitedly*) ... The necklace was too 'hot'. You got the breeze up and persuaded her to take it back. Then realising what an awkward spot you ...
SHERWOOD:	(*Amused*) That isn't daylight you're looking at, Inspector. (*Quietly*) No, I'm sorry to disappoint you, but the necklace wasn't stolen ...
HUDSON:	(*After a tiny pause*) Is that on the level, Tony?
SHERWOOD:	Absolutely.
HUDSON:	Then why did Miss Seaton report that the necklace <u>had</u> been stolen?
SHERWOOD:	Because I – er – persuaded her to do so.
HUDSON:	(*Amazed*) But ... why?
SHERWOOD:	(*Pleasantly*) Do you remember what you said to me about Eric Raynor, Inspector? You said ... "he's pretty cute on turning the tables" ...
HUDSON:	Now what the devil has Raynor got to do with all this?
SHERWOOD:	In the words of that soul stirring ballad, Inspector ... Time alone will tell ...

The door opens. The SERGEANT enters. He is unusually excited.

HUDSON:	What is it, Sergeant?
SERGEANT:	It's Inspector Dixon, sir. He's just picked up Eric Raynort!
HUDSON:	(*Astonished*) … Raynor! What the devil has he been up to?
SERGEANT:	He's been passing forged bank-notes, sir. They're floating all over the West End. The Inspector's almost crazy with excitement.
HUDSON:	(*Staggered*) Forged … bank-notes! But that's not Raynor's racket!!
SERGEANT:	Whether it's his racket or not, sir, the Inspector's got him. He had over three thousand 'snide' notes on him when he was picked up.
HUDSON:	(*Excited*) Phew! Holy mackerel! He'll take the 'rap' this time all right, and no mistake! Tell Inspector Dixon I want to see him.
SERGEANT:	Yes, sir.

The door closes.
There is a pause.

HUDSON:	(*Quietly*) That's funny … I've been after Eric Raynor for twelve years, and then he falls into my lap … just like this …
SHERWOOD:	We'd better have lunch together, eh, Inspector …? Just to celebrate.
HUDSON:	You know, there's something about this Raynor business I don't understand.
SHERWOOD:	Oh, and what's that?
HUDSON:	Where he got the notes from … Somebody must have been damned smart and planted those notes on Raynor …
SHERWOOD:	Now whatever makes you think that, Inspector?

27

HUDSON: Forgery wasn't Eric Raynor's 'racket', I'm
               sure of that.
SHERWOOD: What was his 'racket' …? (*Politely*)
               Turning the tables …?
And ANTHONY SHERWOOD laughs.
FADE IN music.

END OF EPISODE ONE

Episode Two

The Man With
The Perfect Alibi

CHARACTERS:

ANTHONY SHERWOOD

MRS DIMBLE (NANNY)

RICKY SHAW

LINDA MARTIN

RAYMOND

2ND WAITER

PERRY WYATT

ED NORTHGATE

CHIEF INSPECTOR HUDSON

MADELINE KENT

Introductory music … Opening announcement …
FADE music

… CROSS FADE with the end of a sophisticated cabaret turn. A burst of applause. FADE IN chatter … the popping of champagne corks … general laughter. The dance orchestra starts … a quiet, sentimental tune. RAYMOND, the HEAD WAITER, arrives at the entrance to the dining-room to greet ANTHONY SHERWOOD.

RAYMOND: (*Pleasantly*) Ah, good evening, Monsieur! Good evening, Madam!

SHERWOOD: Good evening. I believe you have a table reserved for me. The name is Sherwood. Anthony Sherwood.

RAYMOND: But of course … we've been expecting you. This way, Madam!

FADE IN the Dance Orchestra.

MADELINE: We appear to have missed the cabaret, Tony.

RAYMOND: Yes Madam, it's just finished. I hope this table is satisfactory, sir?

SHERWOOD: Supposing it isn't?

RAYMOND: (*A shade surprised*) Well … I'm afraid it's the only one we have left, sir.

SHERWOOD: (*Amused*) That's all right.

2nd WAITER: Cocktail, Madam?

SHERWOOD: What would you like, Madeline?

MADELINE: Er … White Lady?

SHERWOOD: And a Bronx.

RAYMOND: White Lady and a Bronx.

2nd WAITER: Very good, sir.

RAYMOND: (*Suddenly*) Pardon, Monsieur … I'll take your order in a few moments.

A pause.

31

SHERWOOD:	When did you arrive, Madeline?
MADELINE:	Thursday ... on the Normandie.
SHERWOOD:	Thursday? You must have sent me that telegram the moment you landed. Very sweet of you, my dear, although hardly in keeping with your usual technique.
MADELINE:	Pig! No, honestly, Tony, I was terribly worried.
SHERWOOD:	Worried?
MADELINE:	Yes. I'd heard so many rumours. Why, one of the stewards on board actually told me that you'd been murdered!
SHERWOOD:	A slight overstatement, Madeline, I'm glad to say.
MADELINE:	Then when we got the papers at Cherbourg I ...
SHERWOOD:	You read about the accident?
MADELINE:	Accident! There seems to have been a series of them, so far as I can gather.
SHERWOOD:	(*Quietly*) Yes. The first was about a fortnight ago ... the last on Tuesday.
MADELINE:	(*Puzzled*) On Tuesday ...? But what happened ...?
SHERWOOD:	(*Casually*) Oh ... I happened to be in a lift at The Winter Hotel ... one of those self-driven things. The lift shaft gave way and nearly ... anyway, I had to make a jump for it. The whole thing was pretty badly organised.
MADELINE:	Organised! You mean ... it was done deliberately?
SHERWOOD:	Well, three "accidents" in two weeks, darling, it seems to be stretching the arm of co-incidence, doesn't it?

MADELINE:	But whose doing it?
SHERWOOD:	It might be one of so many people, surely you realise that?
MADELINE:	Well, you've only got yourself to blame, Tony. I told you years ago that if you must make easy money, then for heaven's sake pick on respectable people to make it out of …
SHERWOOD:	(*Amused*) Like you, Madeline?
MADELINE:	… Instead of which you made a small fortune out of practically every dangerous character in Europe. People like Eric Raynor neither forgive nor forget, remember that, Tony.
SHERWOOD:	(*Quietly*) It isn't Eric Raynor. I took care of that gentleman weeks ago.
MADELINE:	Then who is it …? You must have some idea?

Tiny pause.

SHERWOOD:	Remember … "Ricky Shaw"?
MADELINE:	(*Surprised*) Ricky Shaw! The man with the perfect alibi! He's not in town, surely.
SHERWOOD:	Isn't he! That's where you're mistaken. Ricky's very much in Town these days. He owns The Winter Hotel, one of the best night clubs in the West End, and according to rumour several less reputable haunts.
MADELINE:	Don't tell me he's going straight?
SHERWOOD:	Not Ricky. But they can't get their hands on him.
MADELINE:	Always the perfect alibi?
SHERWOOD:	Always the perfect alibi.
MADELINE:	How did you find out about Ricky?

SHERWOOD:	Inspector Hudson tipped me off after the lift smash.
MADELINE:	Ricky wasn't responsible for that Hatton Garden job by any chance ... The Franklin Emerald?
SHERWOOD:	Yes ... At least, Hudson seems to think so. Apparently, the safe was a new Duzenburg and there aren't many boys around who can 'crack' that sort of thing. Ricky happens to be one of them. But ... as usual ... he had the perfect alibi.
RAYMOND:	White Lady and a Bronx, Monsieur.
SHERWOOD:	Ah ... thank you.

Tiny pause.

MADELINE:	Well, here's luck, Tony.
SHERWOOD:	Happy days, Madeline!

A pause.

MADELINE:	Tony ...
SHERWOOD:	Yes, dear?
MADELINE:	That night club ... the one you mentioned ... the one that belongs to Ricky Shaw ... what do they call it?
SHERWOOD:	The Five Hundred Club.
MADELINE:	The Five ... (*Staggered*) The Five Hundred Club! But ... this is The Five Hundred Club!!!
SHERWOOD:	But of course, my sweet. (*Casually*) Shall we dance?

FADE IN dance orchestra.

FADE dance music and cross fade with the voices of RICKY SHAW and LINDA MARTIN. RICKY SHAW is an American. Tough, callous, yet not by any means a fool. LINDA MARTIN is an Australian. She is about forty and obviously in love with RICKY.

SHAW: (*Irritated*) It's not a bit of use arguing, Linda! Mendoza played you for a sucker. I ought to have had more sense than to have sent you.

LINDA: But you said the emerald was only worth ten thousand, and when …

SHAW: (*Exasperated*) Ten grand! The Franklin emerald!!! Chee!!!!

LI NDA: (*Suddenly annoyed*) Listen, Ricky, it's always the same when I do anything. But I notice it's always me that's got to do the dirty work. That emerald was hot … red hot … but I carried it from London to Paris to Bucharest … And for what, may I ask? For what?

Tiny pause.

RICKY: (*Chuckling*) OK, Linda … OK honey!

LINDA: If Mendoza lives up to his promise you should get the money in about six weeks. I got just over four thousand on account.

RICKY: Four thousand? Well, I guess it might have been worse. You look as if you can use a drink, Linda?

LINDA: Gin and tonic … and go steady on the tonic, Ricky.

RICKY: OK. (*He mixes the drink*) What sort of a crossing did you have?

LINDA: M'm … fair.

RICKY: Have a good time in Paris?

LINDA: Not bad. I stayed the first two nights with Chinetti.

RICKY: That wop!

LINDA: He may be a 'wop' but he's a gentleman.

RICKY: I wouldn't be knowing. Here's your drink, Linda.

LINDA: Thanks.

35

RICKY: By the way, we had a visitor a couple of days ago, quite a distinguished visitor. Pity you missed him, Linda.

LINDA: Oh, who was that?

RICKY: Chief-Inspector George St John Hudson.

LINDA: (*Anxiously*) Hudson? What happened?

RICKY: Oh, he was quite pleasant, we discussed the Hatton Garden job and of course I ... er ... provided him with my alibi.

LINDA: He knew you'd pulled the job, of course?

RICKY: He must have done. There isn't another guy in Town who can crack a new Duzenburg. Still, he's a smart man Hudson, didn't take him ten seconds to realise my alibi was foolproof.

LINDA: He didn't mention the Sherwood business, by any chance?

RICKY: (*Suddenly annoyed*) Now why the hell mention that rat?

LINDA: Well, did he?

Tiny pause.

RICKY: Yes, as a matter of fact he did. Hudson's got a pretty shrewd suspicion I'm after Sherwood and when that lift shaft collapsed ...

LINDA: That was a damn fool thing to do, if you like!

RICKY: Damn fool thing or not, I'm going to get Sherwood if it takes me ...

LINDA: Listen, Ricky ... Ten years ago Sherwood made a fool out of you, I don't know how much he got out of it, but ...

RICKY: Two hundred grand! Two hundred grand! ... And I was sitting on top of the world, Linda!

LINDA: And you'll be sitting on top of it again, Ricky, if you play your cards properly.

RICKY: Maybe.

LINDA:	Now take my tip and lay off Sherwood, he's dynamite.
RICKY:	OK …

A knock is heard.

RICKY:	Come in!

The door opens.

LINDA:	This is a private office, I suppose you …
SHERWOOD:	(*Pleasantly*) Hello, Ricky!
RICKY:	Say, how the devil did you get in here?
SHERWOOD:	I booked a table.
RICKY:	This office is private, Sherwood, you can read!
SHERWOOD:	Now fancy you remembering!
LINDA:	Sherwood! So this is … Anthony Sherwood?
SHERWOOD:	This is my first visit to The Five Hundred Club, since you took it over. I must compliment you, Ricky. You've made a great difference to the place. I much prefer it to The Winter Hotel. The lift, for one thing, seems much more reliable.
RICKY:	I don't know what the hell you're talking about.
SHERWOOD:	Don't you …? (*Casually*) Could I trouble you for a light? My cigar seems … Ah, thank you, Ricky!
RICKY:	(*After a slight pause*) What is it you want, Sherwood?
SHERWOOD:	But I thought I'd made that quite clear. Just a friendly chat. (*To Linda. Pleasantly*) Would you care for a cigarette? (*Opening his case*) … Turkish … Virginian …?
LINDA:	Thank you. I have my own.

SHERWOOD:	How very nice. Lighter, Ricky! Lighter! Never keep a lady waiting.

SHERWOOD lights LINDA's cigarette.

LINDA:	Thank you.
SHERWOOD:	And how are you these days? Does night life agree with you …? You look very fit, I must confess.
RICKY:	I'm OK …
SHERWOOD:	Splendid! Splendid! I'm glad to hear it.
RICKY:	And how have you been keeping … in good health … I hope?
SHERWOOD:	No … I can't say I have, Ricky. In fact, just between me and you, I've had one or two nasty turns … so nasty that I've decided to … er … do something about it …
RICKY:	(*Quietly*) Is that wise?
SHERWOOD:	(*Amused*) We shall see, Ricky. We shall see.

The telephone rings.

RICKY:	(*Lifting receiver*) Hello? … Yes … Yes … Who is that speaking? … Ed … Who? … Ed Northgate … Oh, yeah … Yeah, I remember … M'm …? No, no, I can't talk over the phone … I might … Not at the moment, but I shall be … Well, come straight up … Yes, that's all right. Ask the head waiter he'll show you … OK … (*Rings off. To SHERWOOD*) You'll have to excuse me, Sherwood. I …
SHERWOOD:	Yes, and you must excuse me too, Ricky. I'm doing the very thing I advised you not to do … Keep a lady waiting. And what a lady! Do you remember Madeline Kent?

	No, you probably wouldn't … Well, I must be off. So glad to have met you Miss … er …?
LINDA:	Martin. Linda Martin.
SHERWOOD:	Linda Martin? We might meet again sometime.
LINDA:	(*Pleasantly*) Why not? It's a small world.

The door closes.

RICKY:	(*Angrily*) I like his nerve! What the hell does he think this joint is? Busting in here as if …
LINDA:	Sherwood's different from what I expected. He's got charm.
RICKY:	If that's what you like to call it. (*Thoughtfully*) I wonder who this guy Northgate is? He seemed pretty 'het up' over the phone.
LINDA:	Don't you know him?
RICKY:	Apparently we met a couple of years ago in Detroit. But I can't place him. (*Puzzled*) Northgate … Northgate … Northgate … (*Suddenly*) I've got him! Say, he used to be in quite a big way of business …

The door opens. PERRY WYATT enters. He is about thirty-eight.

PERRY:	Ricky, I thought perhaps you'd like to know … (*Surprised*) Hello, Linda! When did you get back?
LINDA:	About an hour ago.
RICKY:	What is it, Perry?
PERRY:	Anthony Sherwood's downstairs. He's having dinner with …
RICKY:	(*Impatiently*) Yes, yes, I've seen him.
PERRY:	(*Surprised*) You've seen him!

LINDA: He came up here a few minutes ago. I've told
            Ricky to lay off Sherwood, it's a damn sight too
            risky.
PERRY: I agree. It's no good letting personal feelings run
            away with you. Not at a time like this. What
            happened, Linda, about the …
RICKY: She got ten grand.
PERRY: Ten thousand! Phew! Not bad.
There is a knock on the door.
PERRY: (*Startled*) Who's this …?
RICKY: It's all right, there's no need to get jumpy!
LINDA: It's probably Northgate.
RICKY: Yes. (*Calling*) Come in!
*The door opens. ED NORTHGATE is about thirty. Suave, and
well dressed.*
ED: May I come in? Ah, hello, Ricky … How very
            nice to see you again. Now don't say you don't
            remember?
RICKY: (*Breezily*) Chee! Of course I remember! Detroit
            … 1934. The Paradise Club. (*Pleasantly*) Sit
            down, Ed! Sit down!
ED: Actually, I haven't a great deal of time on my
            hands, but …
RICKY: What would you like? A whisky an' soda?
ED: That would do admirably.
RICKY: Whisky an' soda, Perry. Make mine a Bronx.
            Well, Ed, how long have you been over here?
ED: About two months.
RICKY: Everything … er … turning up to …
            expectations?
ED: So far.
RICKY: Swell. (*Taking the drinks from PERRY*) Ah,
            thanks, Perry.
ED: (*Taking a glass*) Thank you.

RICKY: (*Drinking*) Skoal!

A tiny pause.

ED: I read about the Franklin emerald, Ricky. That
           was a splendid piece of work.

RICKY: I don't get you?

ED: Possibly not ... but you got the emerald.

PERRY: (*Angry*) What the hell business of yours ...

RICKY: Quiet, Perry! (*Tiny pause*) Say, what is this?

ED: Are these people friends ... real friends?

RICKY: Absolutely! You can talk.

ED: (*Quietly, with confidence*) The Franklin emerald
           was stolen. It was stolen by a gentleman who has
           an intimate knowledge of the somewhat involved
           intricacies of a Duzenburg safe. Now, strange
           though it may seem there are only two men in
           Europe who can, to put it vulgarly 'crack' a
           Duzenburg. A gentleman by the name of Otto
           Wanger and a certain Mr Ricky Shaw. Now Otto
           happens to be in Vienna, and Vienna ... even as
           the proverbial crow flies ... is a very, very long
           way from Hatton Garden ...

RICKY: I had an alibi! A water tight alibi! And if you
           think ...

ED: My dear Ricky, of course you had an alibi! But
           the point is ...

RICKY: (*Tensely*) The point is this! What's on your
           mind?

ED: It's a long story ... but I'll be brief. An
           acquaintance of mine has a house, a rather
           charming house in Berkeley Square. He also has
           a rather charming, and I must confess, a rather
           priceless collection of diamonds. Now he keeps
           these diamonds in a safe ... a Duzenburg safe ...

41

RICKY:	(*Quickly*) So that's the racket! What are they worth?
ED:	About twenty-seven thousand … pounds.
RICKY:	Chee!
LINDA:	Who is this friend?
ED:	Lord Abingdale. Modesty forbids me calling him a friend but …
RICKY:	(*Excitedly*) Twenty-seven thousand!
ED:	At a conservative estimate.
RICKY:	What's your proposition?
ED:	Tomorrow afternoon His Lordship, together with his personal secretary and most of the staff, leave for the Isle of Wight. This leaves the town house and consequently the diamonds, in the care of a certain Mr Jukes. Mr Jukes is old and can, I assure you, very easily be taken care of. I would suggest therefore that at about a quarter to twelve tomorrow evening we … that is, you and I, Ricky … visit Berkeley Square and …
RICKY:	(*Interrupting*) Seems a pretty sound set-up. What do you think, Linda?
LINDA:	What's the 'cut' …?
ED:	Ah, yes … the 'cut'. Well, the safe, of course, would be your headache, Ricky, and although naturally I …
RICKY:	Listen! Supposing I take the proposition over … 'crack' the Duzenburg and 'fence' the stuff?
ED:	Then what do I get out of it?
RICKY:	You know the house?
ED:	Inside out.
RICKY:	Stick with me on the job tomorrow night, and I'll cut you in for five thousand.
ED:	Make it ten.

Tiny pause.

RICKY: (*Suddenly*) OK … OK …

PERRY: It's risky, just after the Franklin business.

RICKY: Nonsense! (*With enthusiasm*) Now listen, Perry,
            you round the boys up. I want the house
            completely surrounded by ten thirty tomorrow
            night. Ed, I'll pick you up at …

ED: (*Surprised*) House surrounded? What's the idea?

RICKY: We don't go near the joint until the coast is
            absolutely clear. The boys will give us the tip.

ED: Good. The house is 47A. It's a double fronted
            house with a small terrace overlooking the
            square. We may need an alibi, Ricky, so if I were
            you …

PERRY: You can't teach Ricky anything about alibis.

ED: No, no, of course not.

RICKY: (*Thoughtfully*) Berkeley Square. M'm … You've
            got a brother out Romford way, haven't you,
            Perry?

PERRY: That's right. He owns a roadhouse … "The
            Wishing Well".

RICKY: (*Quietly*) Romford … that seems a pretty good
            distance. I don't see how a guy could be at
            Romford and Berkeley Square at the same time,
            do you, Linda?

LINDA: Ricky Shaw might do it.

RICKY: (*Amused*) About this brother of yours, Perry …
            can he be trusted?

PERRY: Absolutely … if it's worth his while.

RICKY: Good. Book me a private room for tomorrow
            night and dinner for two. About eight o'clock,
            Linda, take my Chrysler out to Romford. Leave
            the car parked outside the roadhouse then get
            back here. As soon as you get back start putting
            on an act in the restaurant. You know the sort of

43

	stuff … I've left you high and dry for some dizzy blonde. Tell the whole place I'm having one hell of a good time with her out at Romford.
LINDA:	OK.
RICKY:	Pile the jealous lover stuff on for all you're worth, don't be frightened of overdoing it. Then, if anything does go wrong, Perry's brother will …
PERRY:	Don't worry, Carl will back you up all right. I'll see to that.
RICKY:	Good. Then we'd better meet tomorrow, Ed, say about ten-thirty. That should give you plenty of time to fix an alibi.
ED:	Ten-thirty? Splendid! Then until tomorrow … au revoir!

The door closes.

Tiny pause.

PERRY:	What do you make of that fellow, Ricky?
RICKY:	He's all right. There can't be any double-cross, if that's what you're thinking.
LINDA:	I wouldn't be so sure.
RICKY:	How can there be? Ed would have done the job himself, if the safe hadn't been a Duzenburg, that's obvious. In any case, he's still going to be in on it … and I'll see he's in the house all the time, don't you worry. Give me a cigarette, Linda.
PERRY:	I'd better give Carl a ring.
RICKY:	(*Casually*) Where's my cigarette lighter? I had it a few minutes ago.
LINDA:	Isn't it on the desk?
RICKY:	I don't see it. (*He is searching for the lighter*) I hope I haven't lost it … it's rather a good one … got my initials on too …

44

PERRY:	Is this it? Oh, no … I'm sorry, it isn't.
RICKY:	I had it when Sherwood was here because … (*Suddenly*) Say, he took it off me and offered you a light, didn't he?
LINDA:	Yes.
RICKY:	I don't remember seeing it again … (*Rather bewildered*) That's funny … Damn funny!

FADE IN music.

FADE DOWN music and FADE IN ANTHONY SHERWOOD knocking on the door of his flat. The door opens.

NANNY:	(*Slightly breathless*) Why on earth don't you …
SHERWOOD:	Ah, the dragon herself … What's the idea of bolting the door, Nanny?
NANNY:	The door wasn't bolted! It wasn't even locked! (*Surprised*) Hello, my lad … are you tipsy?
SHERWOOD:	Mrs Dimble … you forget yourself!
NANNY:	Fine time of night to be … Here, let me have your coat …
SHERWOOD:	Ah, thank you, Mrs Dimble. Thank you!
NANNY:	You'll find a plate of sandwiches on the cocktail cabinet.
SHERWOOD:	Excellent!
NANNY:	(*With a sigh*) I don't know what you'd do without me!
SHERWOOD:	Madeline sends her love, Nanny.
NANNY:	(*Puzzled*) Madeline …?
SHERWOOD:	Madeline Kent. You remember … Tall … Blonde … and surprisingly intelligent.
NANNY:	(*Thoughtfully*) Madeline Kent …? Was that the girl in Buenos Aires … the one

	with a delightful mother? Remember, we left rather hurriedly after ...
SHERWOOD:	No, darling, that was not Madeline ... Her name was Maisie ... and she was not very intelligent. (*Tiny pause*) M'm – these sandwiches are delicious.
NANNY:	Did everything go off all right tonight?
SHERWOOD:	Fine! No accidents tonight, Nanny! (*Suddenly*) Oh, by the way, have there been any telephone messages for me?
NANNY:	Yes, about an hour ago. A man called Ed Northgate rang up. He left a message.
SHERWOOD:	What did he say?
NANNY:	(*Thoughtfully*) Now let me see ... I wrote it down on a pad so that ... Ah, here we are! He said: "Everything went according to plan, and you'll find the car outside of The Wishing Well roadhouse at Romford ... tomorrow night.
SHERWOOD:	Romford? Good.
NANNY:	I'd no sooner put the telephone down than a man called to see you ... a funny little man who said his name was Tommy Benger.
SHERWOOD:	Tommy Benger! Excellent!
NANNY:	When I said that you were out, he said ... "Tell Mr Sherwood I'll do it ... but it's worth more than fifty quid" ... He said that he'd call round tomorrow ... or rather this morning.
SHERWOOD:	(*Delighted*) Splendid! Good for Tommy!
NANNY:	Tony ... who is this man Benger, and why should ...?

46

SHERWOOD:	(*Interrupting*) He used to be a racing driver at Brooklands. Made quite a name for himself at one time. He went over to America in 1930 and tried his hand at stunt driving … You know the sort of thing … smashing cars to bits and escaping by the skin of his teeth. He's got plenty of nerve although you'd never dream of it to look at him.
NANNY:	You certainly wouldn't. But why should …
SHERWOOD:	Now, no more questions, Nanny, please!
NANNY:	But, Tony, if this man used to make money out of smashing …
SHERWOOD:	Don't be so curious, Nanny! (*Yawning*) Gosh, I'm ready for bed.

FADE IN music.

FADE music.

A door opens. PERRY WYATT enters.

LINDA:	(*Tensely*) Oh, it's you, Perry!
PERRY:	(*Nervously*) Hasn't he returned yet?
LINDA:	No.
PERRY:	My God, I hope there's been no slip-up.
LINDA:	I'm worried.
PERRY:	He's been gone nearly nine hours, it's unlike Ricky.
LINDA:	What time did you and the boys leave?
PERRY:	About five. It was almost daylight.
LINDA:	I don't suppose he could have left the house without …
PERRY:	(*Impatiently*) No, no, impossible. One of us would certainly have spotted him. (*Suddenly*) Here's Ricky!

47

The door opens. RICKY SHAW is breathless and rather excited.

RICKY: Hello, Perry! Hello sweet, you look worried!

LINDA: What happened?

RICKY: The safe was a swine. It took me five hours to get the combination straight. Mix me a drink, Linda.

PERRY: Where's Northgate?

RICKY: He left me at the house. We thought it best. That boy was a pip! He stayed with me on the job from start to finish.

PERRY: (*Anxiously*) But whose got the stuff?

RICKY: (*Amused*) Chee, I'm not that crazy! It's right here.

LINDA: What are they like?

RICKY: They look terrific, but you're the best judge of diamonds, Sugar.

PERRY: You've got a nerve, driving through the streets with that wad.

RICKY: Did you plant the alibi ok …?

LINDA: Yes. I took the car out to Romford straight away … and did I put on an act in the restaurant!

PERRY: She nearly convinced me that … (*He stops speaking*)

There is a pause.

RICKY: (*Quietly*) What is it, Linda?

PERRY: (*Anxiously*) What's the matter?

LINDA: Is this the stuff you got from the house in Berkeley Square?

RICKY: Why, of course!

LINDA starts to laugh. She is obviously amused.

RICKY: Linda!

PERRY: What the hell is the matter?

LINDA:	(*Scornfully*) It's paste! Paste! The whole lot isn't worth more than a fiver.
RICKY:	You're crazy!!!
LINDA:	(*Calmly*) All right, Ricky, I'm crazy. But I know diamonds when I see them … when I see them.
RICKY:	Is this on the level?
LINDA:	Absolutely.
RICKY:	Chee!
PERRY:	(*Desperately*) Northgate must be in on this …
RICKY:	(*Thoughtfully*) Yeah …
PERRY:	What's the racket …?
RICKY:	I don't know.
LINDA:	Was there anything else in the safe?
RICKY:	Not a thing. That rather surprised me because … (*He is interrupted by the telephone ringing*)
PERRY:	I'll take it. (*Lifts the receiver*) Hello … Oh, hello, Ray … Yes …? (*Desperately*) Thanks … That's all right. (*He replaces the receiver*)
RICKY:	What is it?
PERRY:	Hudson! He's on his way up here …
RICKY:	My God, that's quick work … Get out of here, Perry … You too, Linda … I'll handle this. Take this damn stuff with you!
PERRY:	OK … Come on, Linda.
LINDA:	We'll see you later, Ricky.
RICKY:	(*Thoughtfully*) Yeah …

The door closes. RICKY mixes himself a drink. A knock is heard.

RICKY:	Come in …

The door opens.

HUDSON:	Hello, Ricky.
RICKY:	(*Brightly*) Hello, Inspector. Come in.

HUDSON:	(*Breathless*) It's quite a climb up those stairs. It beats me why …
RICKY:	What you need is a drink. I'll fix it.
HUDSON:	(*Quietly*) I'm sorry, Ricky. This isn't a friendly call.
RICKY:	What do you mean?
HUDSON:	I've got a warrant out for … your arrest.
RICKY:	Well, this isn't the first time.
HUDSON:	No, but it's going to be the last.
RICKY:	I wouldn't be too sure of that, if I were you, Hudson.
HUDSON:	Always the perfect alibi, eh, Ricky? Where were you between the hours of … er … eight o'clock last night, and seven this morning?
RICKY:	I left here about eight o'clock and went out to Romford. I stayed the night at …
HUDSON:	(*Staggered*) Romford!
RICKY:	(*Calmly*) Sure … Romford. There's nothing funny about that, is there?
HUDSON:	(*Amused*) Well, it just depends which way you look at it.
RICKY:	What do you mean?
HUDSON:	Let's get this straight … You left here last night for Romford … in a car … a Chrysler … FKY 763?
RICKY:	That's right.
HUDSON:	(*Bewildered*) You admit it?
RICKY:	Absolutely. (*Puzzled*) Say, what is this?
HUDSON:	Well, to be quite truthful, "this" is somewhat in the nature of a surprise, Ricky. You see, we know that you went out to Romford, we know that you stayed the night there … but we certainly never thought that you'd admit it.
RICKY:	Admit it? (*Amused*) Why shouldn't I admit it?

HUDSON:	(*Softly*) This charge is serious, Ricky. Pretty serious. Attempted murder … always is.
RICKY:	(*Amazed*) Attempted murder! Chee, are you crazy?
HUDSON:	You've been trying to get Anthony Sherwood for a long time, Ricky, but last night you over-stepped the mark.
RICKY:	Last night!
HUDSON:	I suppose you don't know what happened? I suppose your memory doesn't recall a little incident on the main Ilford road?
RICKY:	(*Bewildered*) … On the main Ilford road …?
HUDSON:	It took a hell of a nerve driving straight at Sherwood, I'll say that for you, Ricky. Still, thank God you missed him!
RICKY:	… Driving straight at … Sherwood … (*Suddenly desperate*) Say, Hudson … listen. I've been framed. I never went near Romford last night. I swear to …
HUDSON:	Oh! Oh! That's rich. My dear Ricky, we've got more evidence than we know what to do with. Firstly, your car was recognised. Secondly, Linda Martin told practically the whole town you were out at Romford. And thirdly, there's this little gadget …
RICKY:	My cigarette lighter! Where did you find that?
HUDSON:	Believe it or not, Ricky, by the side of your car.
RICKY:	By … the … side of my car …? Chee!
HUDSON:	For the first time in your life, Ricky, you haven't got a leg to stand on.

FADE IN music.

FADE and slowly CROSS FADE with the end of the opening cabaret turn: a burst of applause; FADE IN chatter; the popping of champagne corks ... general laughter ... the dance orchestra starts ... a quiet sentimental tune. RAYMOND, the HEAD WAITER, arrives at the entrance to the dining room to greet ANTHONY SHERWOOD.

RAYMOND: (*Pleasantly*) Ah, good evening, Monsieur. Good evening, Madam.

SHERWOOD: Good evening. I believe you have a table reserved for me. My name is Sherwood. Anthony Sherwood.

RAYMOND: But of course ... we've been expecting you. This way, Madam.

FADE IN the dance orchestra.

MADELINE: We appear to have missed the cabaret, Tony.

RAYMOND: Yes, Madam, it's just finished. I hope this table is satisfactory, sir?

SHERWOOD: Supposing it isn't?

RAYMOND: (*A shade surprised*) Well ... I'm afraid it's the only one we have left, sir.

SHERWOOD: (*Amused*) That's all right.

2nd WAITER: Cocktail, Madam?

SHERWOOD: What would you like, Madeline?

MADELINE: Er ... White Lady.

SHERWOOD: ... And a Bronx.

RAYMOND: White Lady and a Bronx.

2nd WAITER: Very good, sir.

RAYMOND: (*Suddenly*) Pardon, Monsieur ... I'll take your order in a few moments.

Pause.

SHERWOOD: Well, Madeline, I suppose you read about Ricky Shaw?

MADELINE: Yes. (*Tiny pause*) Ten years seems rather a long time, Tony, for attempted murder.

SHERWOOD: Don't forget he made several attempts.

52

MADELINE:	(*Puzzled*) You know, there's something about that Romford business I don't quite understand.
SHERWOOD:	And what's that, Madeline?
MADELINE:	Well, if Ricky did attempt to murder you … at Romford I mean … why didn't he take the trouble to provide himself with an alibi?
SHERWOOD:	Oh, but he did!
MADELINE:	Then why on earth didn't he use it?
SHERWOOD:	You'd better ask Ricky.
Tiny pause.	
MADELINE:	Tony … how do you know Ricky Shaw had an alibi?
SHERWOOD:	Because I took the trouble to provide him with one.
MADELINE:	(*Amazed*) You … took … the … trouble to provide him with one?
SHERWOOD:	Yes, darling.
MADELINE:	Tony … I … don't understand.
SHERWOOD:	Don't you, my sweet? It's really quite simple. You see, for the first time in his life Ricky Shaw had an alibi. The perfect alibi!!!

And ANTHONY SHERWOOD laughs …
FADE IN music.

END OF EPISODE TWO

Episode Three

The Prince of Rogues

CHARACTERS:

ANTHONY SHERWOOD

MRS DIMBLE (NANNY)

CHIEF INSPECTOR HUDSON

LYDIA

ANGELO

COUNTESS MANNERHEIM

BENSON

PAGE BOY

WAITER

CONCIERGE

Introductory music … Opening announcement …
FADE music

*… FADE IN the noise of people laughing, chatting … in the
background the Casino orchestra are playing a sentimental
waltz. Above the noise of the conversation can be heard the
coaxing voices of the croupiers.*

SHERWOOD: (*Pleasantly*) Hello, Mrs Dimble!
NANNY: Hello, Tony! Where on earth have you
              been? I've been looking all over the casino
              for you.
SHERWOOD: Don't lie. Nanny! You've had your eyes
              positively glued to the tables ever since
              you arrived.
NANNY: I can't understand it, Tony. My system
              was perfectly all right on paper. It worked
              beautifully.
SHERWOOD: How much have you lost?
NANNY: About five hundred francs. (*Anxiously*)
              But don't worry, I'll get it back.
SHERWOOD: (*Amused*) Come along, Nanny, let's have a
              cocktail. Then, if you're a good girl, you
              can try your luck at chemin-de-fer.
NANNY: Chemin-de … fer …? Doesn't sound very
              decent to me! Still, I'll try anything once!
SHERWOOD laughs. They have arrived at the cocktail bar.
ANGELO: Good evening … Monsieur Sherwood …
              it is nice to see you back in Monte Carlo
              again …
SHERWOOD: Thank you, Angelo … It's nice to be back
              … What would you like, Nanny?
NANNY: Er … Pink champagne …

57

SHERWOOD: Pink Champagne! It seems to me it's a
               great pity you ever saw Irene Dunne in
               Love Affair. Two champagne cocktails,
               Angelo!
ANGELO: Merci, Monsieur!
Tiny pause.
SHERWOOD: Well, Nanny ... enjoying your holiday?
NANNY: Oh, it's lovely, Tony.
SHERWOOD: Tomorrow we'll hire a car and ride over to
               San Remo, then later in the ... (*He stops
               speaking*)
NANNY: What is it, Tony?
SHERWOOD: There's that girl, Nanny. The one that was
               on the train ... the one with the dark
               glasses ... remember?
NANNY: Yes. She still seems rather worried about
               something, doesn't she?
SHERWOOD: (*Thoughtfully*) Yes.
ANGELO: (*Suddenly*) Two champagne cocktails,
               Monsieur.
SHERWOOD: Ah!
NANNY: Pink champagne?
ANGELO: (*Amused*) Pink champagne, Madam!
*They all laugh. Their glasses touch. A note is thrown on to the
cocktail bar.*
SHERWOOD: Keep the change, Angelo!
ANGELO: Merci, Monsieur!
Tiny pause.
NANNY: (*Softly*) Why don't you ask him, Tony? –
               You're obviously dying to find out who
               she is!
SHERWOOD is amused.
SHERWOOD: (*Calling*) Angelo!

58

ANGELO:	(*From the opposite end of the cocktail bar*) Monsieur!
SHERWOOD:	(*Quietly*) Have you any idea who that girl is … the one in the white dress, and wearing the dark glasses …?
ANGELO:	I don't know for certain, Monsieur. I have heard a rumour that she is Lydia Van Tyler, but whether it is true or not, I cannot say. She is staying at the Palace Hotel … quite alone, I believe.
SHERWOOD:	Thank you, Angelo.
NANNY:	(*Staggered*) Lydia Van Tyler!!! But … isn't she the richest girl in the world?
SHERWOOD:	Well, one of them … if not the richest. Got quite a reputation for loathing publicity. Why, they do say that when she arrived in New York for the … (*Softly*) Hello, she's going out on to the terrace.
NANNY:	(*Alarmed*) Tony!
SHERWOOD:	What is it?
NANNY:	She … took something out of her handbag. It looked to me like a revolver. Oh, but that's silly of me! It couldn't possibly have been a …
SHERWOOD:	(*Quietly*) Wait here, Nanny!

FADE IN the casino orchestra.
FADE DOWN to the background.
Somewhere in the distance can be heard the faint rolling of the sea.

SHERWOOD:	(*Calmly*) I wouldn't do that if I were you!
LYDIA:	(*Startled*) Oh!
SHERWOOD:	I'm sorry if I startled you. Here, let me take care of that …

59

LYDIA:	(*Intensely annoyed*) Please leave me alone!
SHERWOOD:	With pleasure … once you've handed over the revolver.
LYDIA:	I should esteem it a favour if you would kindly mind your own business!
SHERWOOD:	Miss Van Tyler, as a firm … and somewhat fervent … believer in disarmament, I must insist! The revolver … (*Tiny pause*) Thank you.
LYDIA:	Now, will you please leave me alone?
SHERWOOD:	(*Calmly*) Of course. Good night.
LYDIA:	(*Surprised*) Oh, I … didn't mean to be rude.
SHERWOOD:	Didn't you? Then that makes a difference. Cigarette?
LYDIA:	(*Both amused and amazed*) I say, you are an unusual sort of person, aren't you?

Tiny pause.

SHERWOOD:	(*Quietly*) Is this thing loaded?
LYDIA:	Yes.
SHERWOOD:	Then you did intend to …?
LYDIA:	Yes.
SHERWOOD:	Judged from conventional standards that seems to make you a rather unusual sort of person too, doesn't it?
LYDIA:	(*Slightly amused*) Yes, I suppose it does. (*Seriously*) I don't know why I'm laughing, I'm sure, there's nothing very funny about it. It's really … rather tragic. By the way, you called me Miss Van Tyler just now, how did you know my name?
SHERWOOD:	Someone told me …
LYDIA:	You're Anthony Sherwood, aren't you?

SHERWOOD:	Yes.
LYDIA:	I've heard a great deal about you.
SHERWOOD:	Complimentary, I hope?
LYDIA:	Not all of it, I'm afraid. A woman I met at Nice said that you were the Prince of Rogues.
SHERWOOD:	Was she tall and stout and very domineering?
LYDIA:	Yes. How did you know?
SHERWOOD:	She sounds as if she might have been.
LYDIA:	(*After a tiny pause*) I suppose you are wondering why I attempted to commit suicide?
SHERWOOD:	The thought had crossed my mind.
LYDIA:	It's not a very original story, I'm afraid.
SHERWOOD:	Don't forget this is the casino terrace at Monte Carlo, it's not a very original setting.

LYDIA laughs.

| SHERWOOD: | Why are you laughing? |
| LYDIA: | You forgot to mention the sentimental music. |

Tiny pause.

LYDIA:	I think I will have that cigarette after all.
SHERWOOD:	Yes, of course. (*He lights her cigarette*)
LYDIA:	Thank you. (*Suddenly*) Mr Sherwood, thanks for what you did, about the revolver, I mean. It was really rather stupid of me.
SHERWOOD:	That's all right. We're all rather stupid at times. I once fell in love with a masseuse. (*As an afterthought*) Not a very good masseuse, of course.

61

LYDIA:	(*Laughing*) Of course. (*Suddenly Lydia stops laughing*).
SHERWOOD:	Are you terribly unhappy?
LYDIA:	Not unhappy … exactly. Terribly … desperately … worried.
SHERWOOD:	Why?
LYDIA:	Well … (*She hesitates, then suddenly makes up her mind to confide*) … you've probably read in the newspapers that I'm engaged to marry a man named Louis Mannerheim …
SHERWOOD:	Count Mannerheim …?
LYDIA:	Yes. We're both very much in love and terribly happy, but unfortunately before I met Louis, I was engaged to an American named Hamilton … Cedric Hamilton. I was young and emotional, and … well, I'm afraid I wrote rather a lot of letters. Stupid … sentimental … letters …
SHERWOOD:	I see.
LYDIA:	Louis is a perfect dear. The kindest and sweetest man you could ever wish to meet. But he is nevertheless, and I don't deceive myself on this point, an extremely jealous sort of person. The very mention of Hamilton sends him into …
SHERWOOD:	(*Interrupting*) Is Hamilton blackmailing you?
LYDIA:	Yes. (*Suddenly*) But he's not demanding money! Oh, no, he's far too subtle for that. He wants me to return … to him …
SHERWOOD:	M'm, sounds a pleasant sort of individual.
LYDIA:	He's staying at The Carlton. I saw him for a few moments tonight … but it's quite

	hopeless ... he won't listen to reason. I'm afraid he'll show Louis the ...
SHERWOOD:	Is your fiancé in Monte Carlo?
LYDIA:	No. He's in Paris on business. I'm supposed to be joining him there on Thursday.
SHERWOOD:	How many letters did you write to Hamilton, do you remember?
LYDIA:	Oh yes. I remember all right. Fourteen. As a matter of fact he showed them to me tonight ... at least he showed me the casket.
SHERWOOD:	The casket?
LYDIA:	Yes, he always kept my letters locked in a casket ... a sort of Oriental deed-box. You know the sort of thing ... A large Chinese dragon on the lid, and a lot of strange writing all ...
SHERWOOD:	(*Thoughtfully*) Yes ... I know the sort of thing ... (*Suddenly*) Hello, Nanny!!!
NANNY:	Hello, Tony! I was beginning to wonder what on earth had ...
SHERWOOD:	Miss Van Tyler ... May I introduce Mrs Dimble? My housekeeper, friend, guardian, and general bodyguard ... in fact technically described as 'a treasure'.
NANNY:	How do you do?
LYDIA:	How do you do?
SHERWOOD:	Well, shall we all go and have a cocktail?
LYDIA:	Yes, that might be quite a good idea.

FADE IN slightly of casino orchestra.
Tiny pause.

SHERWOOD:	(*Quietly*) Do you know a restaurant on the Grande Corniche ... Café de Madrid?

LYDIA:	I've heard of it … they say it's very lovely. Why?
SHERWOOD:	Do you think your fiancé would mind terribly if we had dinner together … tomorrow night … say at eight?
LYDIA:	Well, I don't know. Don't forget, he's of a very jealous disposition.
SHERWOOD:	Yes, but don't forget … he's in Paris.

They laugh.

FADE IN of casino orchestra.

FADE DOWN casino orchestra and CROSS-FADE with a small restaurant orchestra at the Café de Madrid. The orchestra are playing a gay romantic melody.

LYDIA:	(*Rather breathless*) I'm terribly sorry I'm late.
SHERWOOD:	Oh, that's all right.
LYDIA:	(*Gazing across the balcony*) Isn't this heavenly!
SHERWOOD:	I've ordered dinner. What would you like to drink … to start with I mean?
LYDIA:	Gin and Italian.
SHERWOOD:	Gin and Italian.
WAITER:	Merci, Monsieur!
LYDIA:	I think this is one of the loveliest restaurants I … (*Surprised*) Hello, what's this?
SHERWOOD:	Oh, just a little present for you.
LYDIA:	(*Puzzled*) A little present …? (*Suddenly*) Good gracious, it … it … isn't … the casket?
SHERWOOD:	I only meant to bring you the letters, but the casket was locked, my time was rather limited and …

LYDIA: (*Laughing*) No wonder they call you …
The Prince of Rogues …

FADE IN restaurant orchestra.

Slow FADE DOWN of music.
A telephone is ringing. The receiver is lifted.

SHERWOOD: Hello? … Yes …? (*Surprised*) Hello!!! …
Well, if it isn't George St John Hudson!
How are you Inspector? … What? …
Why, of course … Come right up! …
M'm? … No, I've been back about a week
… Quiet … You know …Yes, Monte
Carlo … (*Playfully*) Why, Inspector, you
know I never gamble! (*Laughingly*) Yes,
of course … OK … (*Replaces receiver*)

NANNY: Now what does he want?

SHERWOOD: Most probably a whisky and soda. Is that
tonight's paper?

NANNY: No, it's almost a week old. (*Irritated*)
What are you looking for, Tony?

SHERWOOD: I'm looking for those cigars. You
remember, the ones that nearly made me
… (*He pauses*)

NANNY: (*Quietly, obviously surprised*) Tony!

SHERWOOD: What is it. Nanny?

NANNY: Listen … Listen to this … (*Reading*) "A
novel feature of Countess Mannerheim's
party held at The Dorchester Hotel last
night was the first appearance in Europe of
Velsina, the celebrated negro dancer, who
recently appeared before Mr and Mrs
Roosevelt at a party given in their honour
by the British Ambassador. It will be
recalled that Countess Mannerheim was

65

formerly Lydia Van Tyler, and that her marriage to Count Louis Mannerheim only became known to readers of The Evening Post on Tuesday of this week."

SHERWOOD: What's the date on that paper?

NANNY: Saturday … December 28th … (*Surprised*) But, Tony … she couldn't have been at that party … that was the night you went to The Café Madrid, the night you …

A knock is heard on the door.

SHERWOOD: (*Chuckling*) Here's the Inspector!

INSPECTOR: I … I don't understand ..?

SHERWOOD: Don't you, Mrs Dimble?

A second knock is heard.

SHERWOOD: Jump to it, Nanny, jump to it! Never keep a policeman waiting!!!

The door is opened.

HUDSON: Hello, old boy! Hello, Mrs Dimble! My word, you look fit, Sherwood.

SHERWOOD: Yes, that month in Monte Carlo did me the world of good.

HUDSON: A month in Monte Carlo! T't … and they say crime doesn't pay!

SHERWOOD: Is this a friendly call?

HUDSON: But of course, aren't all my calls friendly? I haven't a warrant if that's what you're thinking.

SHERWOOD: Then … what would you like to drink? A whisky and soda … sherry …?

HUDSON: I think I'd rather like a spot of brandy, Tony.

SHERWOOD: Excellent.

NANNY: It's all right, dear, I'll see to it.

SHERWOOD: I'll have a sherry, Nanny.

66

Pause.

HUDSON:	Cigarette?
SHERWOOD:	Thanks. (*He lights the cigarettes*) You look worried, Inspector.
HUDSON:	Yes, I feel worried.
SHERWOOD:	Why? What's the matter?
HUDSON:	Don't you ever read the papers?
SHERWOOD:	Only when I'm ill. I haven't been ill for six months.
HUDSON:	M'm!
NANNY:	Here's your drink, Inspector. Here we are, Tony!
SHERWOOD:	Thanks.
HUDSON:	Ah, your very good health, Mrs Dimble!
NANNY:	Thank you, sir.

A pause.

SHERWOOD:	Well, what is it, George? What's all the fuss about?
HUDSON:	Tony, do you know anything about a girl who calls herself … amongst other things … Princess Inescourt?
SHERWOOD:	Princess Inescourt? No, why do you ask?
HUDSON:	Well, she's certainly got us guessing at the Yard.
SHERWOOD:	What's her racket?
HUDSON:	What isn't her racket! Practically everything in the confidence line. And is that girl smart? Phew! Listen, Tony, you know as well as I do that all this sort of stuff you read in books about people disguising themselves to look like someone else is just so much ballyhoo. But this girl is different. She doesn't

67

	impersonate a person … she literally is that person … it's absolutely uncanny!
NANNY:	(*Excitedly*) Why, Tony! This explains everything! The girl you …
SHERWOOD:	Princess Inescourt, from what you say, Inspector, sounds a very remarkable sort of person.
HUDSON:	Remarkable? I'd like you to meet her, Tony. (*Amused at the thought*) Boy, that would be a day! Princess Inescourt meets Anthony Sherwood, the Prince of Rogues!!!
SHERWOOD:	(*Quietly*) Oh, but we … er … have met, Inspector.
HUDSON:	(*Astonished*) You … have … met? Where?
SHERWOOD:	(*Casually*) Oh … in the moonlight … on a terrace … in Monte Carlo.
HUDSON:	(*Puzzled*) In the moonlight … on a terrace … in Monte … (*Suddenly laughing*) I never know when you're pulling my leg, Tony!

HUDSON roars with laughter, and after a little while ANTHONY SHERWOOD laughs too. But it is not for the same reason.

FADE IN music.

FADE DOWN and slowly CROSS FADE with COUNTESS MANNERHEIM playing the piano. She is playing Debussy's Reflects dans L'eau. She plays with accuracy but without inspiration. Suddenly a door opens and the piano stops.

| COUNTESS: | (*Irritated*) What is it, Benson? I thought I'd made it perfectly clear that I didn't wish to be disturbed! (*The COUNTESS speaks with a slight American accent*). |

BENSON:	I'm very sorry, Madam. But there's a gentleman to see you … he says it's very urgent.
COUNTESS:	But didn't you tell him I wasn't at home?
BENSON:	Yes, Madam, but it didn't seem to have the desired effect.
COUNTESS:	Who is he, Benson?
BENSON:	His name is Sherwood, Madam. Anthony Sherwood.
COUNTESS:	(*Interested*) Anthony Sherwood? The name seems familiar?
BENSON:	He is a gentleman with a strange reputation, Madam, if I may say so. It's a well-known fact that in a certain section of Mayfair society they invariably refer to him as … The Prince of Rogues.
COUNTESS:	Not being a member of Mayfair society, Benson – I wouldn't be knowing. However, perhaps you'd be good enough to ask Mr Sherwood to step into the library.
BENSON:	He is already in the library, Madam.
COUNTESS:	Well, in that case, ask him in here.
BENSON:	Very good, Madam.

The door opens.
There is a pause.

SHERWOOD:	(*Politely*) Thank you …
BENSON:	Mr Sherwood, Madam.
COUNTESS:	Thank you. Benson. That will be all.

The door closes.

SHERWOOD:	Countess Mannerheim?
COUNTESS:	Yes.
SHERWOOD:	I don't think we've had the pleasure of meeting before, Countess.

69

COUNTESS:	I don't think so either, and to be quite frank, I have very little time at my disposal.
SHERWOOD:	In which case you would like me to come straight to the point?
COUNTESS:	By all means.

Tiny pause.

SHERWOOD:	I hope you will forgive me if I make a personal observation?
COUNTESS:	That entirely depends on how personal it is.
SHERWOOD:	I see. (*Suddenly*) Countess, you have been married precisely a week. Your husband is kind, generous, and terribly in love. You would in fact be supremely happy if it were not for one small, but nevertheless excessively irritating, factor.
COUNTESS:	What do you mean?
SHERWOOD:	(*Simply*) You are being blackmailed.

There is a tiny pause.

COUNTESS:	How did you know?
SHERWOOD:	It's true isn't it?
COUNTESS:	Yes. Yes, it's quite true. Before my marriage I was of course Lydia Van Tyler and … (*Suspiciously*) Oh, I'm beginning to see daylight! So you're the person behind this blackmailing stunt!
SHERWOOD:	Countess, believe it or not, I'm here to help you. Indeed, I'm here to give you my personal assurance that there is absolutely nothing for you to worry about.
COUNTESS:	Say, is this on the level?
SHERWOOD:	(*Amused*) Absolutely. Now supposing you tell me precisely what happened?

COUNTESS:	Well, I'm afraid it's rather a crazy sort of story. You see, before I married Count Mannerheim I was engaged to an American called Cedric Hamilton. Cedric was a perfect dear, but ... Oh, so frightfully sentimental! Naturally however I was pretty much in love with him at the time. Well, anyway, to cut a long story short I wrote Cedric some letters ... pretty childish and somewhat sentimental letters, I guess. When we broke off our engagement I asked him for the letters back because I knew that if Louis ever saw them – that is my present husband – there'd be an awful lot of explaining to do. Cedric refused to return them however and suddenly became stupidly sentimental about the whole business. He even carried the letters about with him in a funny sort of Chinese casket. Well, last week the letters were stolen ... stolen by a girl who calls herself Princess Inescourt.
SHERWOOD:	Then you've heard from Princess Inescourt?
COUNTESS:	Three days ago. She wants thirty-five thousand pounds.
SHERWOOD:	Phew!
COUNTESS:	... If I don't deliver the money by eight o'clock tonight she threatens to send Louis the letters. And she will too, I know a determined sort of person when I see one!
SHERWOOD:	Well, that's where you're mistaken, Countess! What arrangements did you make with Princess Inescourt?

COUNTESS:	I promised to meet her at the Ritz Hotel. She told me to ask for Room 706.
SHERWOOD:	(*Thoughtfully*) Room ... 706 ...
COUNTESS:	Mr Sherwood, what did you mean when you said that ... there was absolutely nothing for me to worry about?
SHERWOOD:	I meant, my dear Countess, that there is absolutely nothing for you to worry about.
COUNTESS:	But the letters? What about the letters?
SHERWOOD:	The letters, at the present moment, are safely tucked away in my safe. And the safe is a new Duzenburg, and the only gent who can 'crack' a new Duzenburgh is Ricky Shaw, but Ricky Shaw ... like the letters ... is safely tucked away. So ... there's nothing for you to worry about.
COUNTESS:	(*Staggered*) You ... mean ... that you have the letters?
SHERWOOD:	I do. And if you meet me at the Ritz Hotel this evening for supper, say at ten o'clock, I shall be very happy to hand them over to you.
COUNTESS:	Without ... er ... any strings?
SHERWOOD:	Without any strings, Countess ... I promise. Although I hope you won't hold me responsible for a certain proposition which might – er – enter my head at the sight of you in a Molyneaux gown.
COUNTESS:	(*Amazed*) Schiaparelli.
SHERWOOD:	After all, Countess, don't forget, I am The Prince of Rogues.

The COUNTESS laughs.

COUNTESS:	Tell me ... Why do they call you The Prince of Rogues?

SHERWOOD: Well, er … just between ourselves … I once got the better of a politician.

FADE IN music.

FADE DOWN.
FADE IN of hotel noises.

NANNY: We're miles too early, Tony! If you arranged to meet the Countess at ten, why on earth are …
SHERWOOD: I told you to stay at home, you old dragon!
NANNY: Dragon indeed!
SHERWOOD: This is supposed to be a private supper party!
NANNY: I know your private supper parties, my lad!
SHERWOOD: (*Amused*) All right, Nanny! All right!
NANNY: Have you got the letters?
SHERWOOD: (*Casually*) Yes, of course … they're in my pocket.
NANNY: (*Puzzled*) I don't understand this, Tony! First you meet this Princess Inescourt who is impersonating Countess Mannerheim … or Lydia Van Tyler that was … and she persuades you to steal a casket which …
SHERWOOD: Brr! A nasty word!
NANNY: … which contains letters which belong to the real Countess Mannerheim …
SHERWOOD: (*Mockingly*) … or Lydia Van Tyler that was …
NANNY: Then … to crown everything … instead of handing over the letters you simply hand over the empty casket.
SHERWOOD: That's right!

73

NANNY:	Then you must have guessed that the girl in Monte Carlo wasn't the real Lydia Van Tyler?
SHERWOOD:	(*Amused*) Wait in the lounge, Nanny! I'll join you later!
NANNY:	(*Surprised*) Now where are you off to?
SHERWOOD:	(*From the background*) See you later, Nanny!

FADE Scene.

FADE IN noise of elevator. The elevator stops. The door slides open.

| LIFT BOY: | Room 706 … Second door on the left, sir. |
| SHERWOOD: | Thank you. |

FADE IN noise of the elevator.

FADE DOWN.
Pause.
A door opens.

SHERWOOD:	Good evening, Miss Van Tyler, or should I say Princess Inescourt?
LYDIA:	(*Astonished*) What are you doing here?
SHERWOOD:	Remember me? I'm the SOS guy. Damsels in distress a speciality. (*Suddenly*) Ah, I see you still have the casket!
LYDIA:	What is it you want?
SHERWOOD:	Oh, just a friendly chat. I get desperately lonely at times, but surely I explained all that to you at The Café de Madrid.
LYDIA:	I haven't a great deal of time on my hands, and I'm expecting someone, so …
SHERWOOD:	Ah, yes! Countess Mannerheim. Now there's an interesting girl for you! You know, Princess, I don't think your

	impersonation was quite ... er ... tonish enough.
LYDIA:	Don't you? It managed to do the trick all right.
SHERWOOD:	Trick? What ... trick?
LYDIA:	Well, after all, you did get me the letters didn't you?
SHERWOOD:	I got a casket. A very nice one too. It cost me six hundred francs.
LYDIA:	(*Staggered*) Six hundred ... francs!
SHERWOOD:	(*Politely*) Yes, do you think it was too dear?
LYDIA:	(*Completely amazed*) You mean to say that ... this ... isn't the casket with the letters?
SHERWOOD:	Why no, of course not! Haven't you opened it yet?
LYDIA:	(*Weakly*) No ... it's ... locked.
SHERWOOD:	Ah, yes! I insisted on a lock. I remember showing the original casket to the man in the shop and ...
LYDIA:	The ... original ...? Then you did get the letters?
SHERWOOD:	But of course! I'm delivering them to Miss Van Tyler tonight.
LYDIA:	For ... what?
SHERWOOD:	Not for thirty-five thousand pounds, Princess, I assure you. I may be a little old fashioned, but somehow there's a nasty sort of taste about blackmail ... or don't you agree?

A knock is heard. The door opens.

CONCIERGE:	Princess Inescourt?

LYDIA:	Yes … (*Suddenly*) Oh, what lovely flowers!
CONCIERGE:	Shall I put them in the vase, Madam, or …?
LYDIA:	No, it's all right, I'll take them! (*Excitedly*) Aren't they adorable!
CONCIERGE:	I was asked to deliver this card, Madam.
LYDIA:	Thank you!
CONCIERGE:	Here we are …
LYDIA:	Merci, Monsieur.

Door closes.

LYDIA:	Aren't they absolutely … (*Reading*) "From … The Prince of Rogues…"
SHERWOOD:	I hope you're fond of orchids?
LYDIA:	That's really very sweet … very sweet of you.
SHERWOOD:	And you forgive me for not falling for your … er … little plot?
LYDIA:	But of course! (*Suddenly*) Here … take … the casket! It might be useful for keeping cigarettes in …
SHERWOOD:	(*Amused*) If I can get the lock undone!
LYDIA:	Well, after all, you did pay six hundred francs for it!

They laugh.
FADE IN music.

FADE music.
FADE IN hotel noises.

SHERWOOD:	(*Pleasantly*) Hello, Nanny!
NANNY:	My word, you've been a time! I thought you were never coming!
SHERWOOD:	Has Countess Mannerheim arrived?

NANNY:	Not yet. But it's nearly ten. (*Suddenly*) Why … Why good gracious, that's the casket!!!
SHERWOOD:	(*Amused*) Yes, that's right, Nanny.
NANNY:	Tony, did she give it to you … Princess Inescourt?
SHERWOOD:	Yes.
NANNY:	(*Suspiciously*) Tony Sherwood … you didn't fall for her trick in Monte Carlo by any chance and …?
SHERWOOD:	(*Amused*) I'm afraid so, Nanny.
NANNY:	(*Staggered*) But – but the letters …? You don't mean to say they're in … that … casket …?
SHERWOOD:	(*Chuckling*) I'm afraid so, Nanny! I'm afraid so!!! (*Suddenly calling*) Oh, concierge!
CONCIERGE:	Monsieur?
SHERWOOD:	About those orchids. You might – er – charge them to … Room 706.
CONCIERGE:	Room 706. Why, certainly, Monsieur!!

And ANTHONY SHERWOOD laughs.

END OF EPISODE THREE

77

Episode Four

The Man Who
Changed His Mind

CHARACTERS:

ANTHONY SHERWOOD

MRS DIMBLE (NANNY)

CHIEF INSPECTOR HUDSON

LORD HOLBORN

LADY MILNE

JOHNNY WAYNE

A SECRETARY

SID WILTON

TICKET COLLECTOR

BUTLER

Introductory music … Opening announcement …
FADE music slowly

LORD HOLBORN is dictating … He is a man of about sixty-five. Irritable and pompous.

HOLBORN: Er … this is not a time when we should … er … permit any charitable institution to dictate what is … er … fundamentally … er … right or wrong. Surely there can be no doubt in the mind of every good and sane citizen that the … er … organising of a sweepstake such as is contemplated by The International Hospital Fund is an unpardonable sin and should most certainly on no account be permitted by the Government. I state therefore in writing, what I have previously stated from public platforms all over the country, that the plans contemplated by The International Hospital Fund for the holding of a sweepstake should immediately be abandoned, and that the Government should take every … er … step to see that the … er … scourge of gambling … er … should … er …

SECRETARY: (*Rather bored*) How many of these letters do you want sending out, sir?

HOLBORN: (*Amazed at the interruption*) Er – what's that?

SECRETARY: I said … How many of these letters do you want sending …

HOLBORN: (*Tetchily*) Er … Seven! – Times, Telegraph, Mail, Express, Chronicle,

	Herald … and … er … Manchester Guardian.
SECRETARY:	Very good, Your Lordship.
HOLBORN:	Now … er … where what was I? Where was I?

FADE IN music.

FADE DOWN.
ANTHONY SHERWOOD is having breakfast.

SHERWOOD:	Another cup of coffee, please, Nanny.
NANNY:	Just a moment, dearie! Just a moment!
SHERWOOD:	(*Chuckling*) Have you seen this in the paper about Lord Holborn?
NANNY:	I read something about him but I couldn't make head or tail of it.
SHERWOOD:	The old boy has certainly got his back up about this sweepstake idea.
NANNY:	What is it, Tony? What's it all about?
SHERWOOD:	Well, as you know, sweepstakes on a really big scale, even in aid of charity, aren't permitted in this country. I mean … The Irish Sweepstake … and things like that. Well, The International Hospital Fund have been trying to persuade 'the powers that be' to give their consent to the holding of a sweepstake. There's no doubt about it, it's a pretty worthy charity and from one or two things I've heard, the Government are seriously considering the possibility of making an exception. But this fellow Lord Holborn, who by the way, is a pretty influential sort of person, is all against it. In fact, he's got quite a bee in his bonnet about the whole business. You

	know the sort of thing ... "Gambling scourge of mankind" ...
NANNY:	My word, he does sound a cheerful old blighter! And what about the hospitals? I suppose they can go to ruin for all he cares!
SHERWOOD:	I don't think he's given much thought to that side of the question. He's too busy on his ... 'Stop the Sweepstake' campaign. (*Brightly*) Where's that coffee, Mrs Dimble?
NANNY:	Under your nose, dearie!
SHERWOOD:	(*Pleasantly*) Ah, so it is! So it is! (*He drinks*) That's better!
NANNY:	I've never seen anyone drink coffee like you, Tony. You positively wallow in it.

A bell is heard.

SHERWOOD:	Hello ... who's this?
NANNY:	Not one of your lady friends, I hope!
SHERWOOD:	I hardly think so, Nanny, not at this time of the morning.
NANNY:	It might do you good to see one or two of them at this time of the morning.
SHERWOOD:	Why, Nanny!
NANNY:	You know what I mean! (*Fading voice*) All dolled up with paint ... and powder ...

Pause.

The door opens.

NANNY:	Good morning, Inspector.

Voices are heard in the background.

SHERWOOD:	(*Pleasantly*) Why bless my soul! If it isn't Scotland Yard ... Come along in, Inspector!

HUDSON:	Sorry barging in like this, Tony. (*Amused*) It's all right, Mrs Dimble, you needn't look so grim. I haven't come to arrest him!
SHERWOOD:	Take your coat off.
HUDSON:	No. No, I haven't much time to spare.
SHERWOOD:	You'll have a cup of coffee anyway. Another cup, Nanny!
NANNY:	Perhaps the Inspector feels he wouldn't like to risk it!
HUDSON:	I'll try anything once, even your coffee, Mrs Dimble!
SHERWOOD:	Cigarette?
HUDSON:	I'll … er … have a pipe if you've no objection.
SHERWOOD:	Go ahead.
HUDSON:	(*After lighting his pipe*) Hello … I see you've been reading about Holborn.
SHERWOOD:	Yes. He seems to be getting pretty worked up about this sweepstake business, doesn't he?
HUDSON:	(*Amused*) The old boy's always had this kink against gambling. Still, I shouldn't be surprised if he doesn't put the 'tin lid' on this sweepstake idea. Pretty rotten luck if he does. The International Hospital Fund can certainly do with the L.S.D. There's no doubt about that.
SHERWOOD:	What sort of a man is he?
HUDSON:	Who? (*Pulling at his pipe*) Lord Holborn? I've never actually met him, but according to all accounts he's pretty pig headed.
SHERWOOD:	I don't ever remember seeing the fellow.
HUDSON:	I only saw him once and that was about twelve years ago at the Manchester

	Assizes. He sentenced a little chap called Danny O'Hara to a life sentence. (*Reflectively*) Pretty tough sentence I thought at the time.
SHERWOOD:	(*Thoughtfully*) Danny O'Hara …
HUDSON:	Yes. I don't know whether you remember the case or not. O'Hara was a funny little devil. He started off by being a card sharper and then suddenly became ambitious. He derailed a train on the outskirts of Manchester and calmly relieved the passengers of pretty well everything they possessed.
SHERWOOD:	Now I remember! Wasn't there some talk about O'Hara being not quite right in the head?
HUDSON:	Yes, but they were never able to prove it. Anyhow, O'Hara came before Mr Justice Holborn and when the old boy discovered that Danny was an inveterate gambler well … it was all up … so far as Danny O'Hara was concerned.
SHERWOOD:	He would be pleased!
HUDSON:	He was pleased all right. You ought to have heard the uproar in court. (*Amused*) By gad, what O'Hara threatened to do to old man Holborn was nobody's business!
NANNY:	Here's your coffee, Inspector.
HUDSON:	Ah, thank you, Mrs Dimble … thank you.
Tiny pause.	
SHERWOOD:	(*Quietly*) What was it you wanted to see me about?
HUDSON:	Good Lord, yes! I was forgetting all about it! I went to a party last night, Tony and …

SHERWOOD:	By Jove, we are going gay!
HUDSON:	… And I met a woman called Lady Milne. During the course of our conversation, I began to mention your name and she immediately became rather … well … intrigued. I rather gathered, from what she said, that she'd heard of you and was, for some reason or other, anxious to make your acquaintance. When I was leaving she gave me this note, and asked me if I would be good enough to give it to you.
SHERWOOD:	(*Taking the note*) Oh, thanks. (*He opens the note*) M'm … Grosvenor House … (*Reading*) "Dear Mr Sherwood, I should very much like to have the pleasure of meeting you, and if you can manage to call round and see me one afternoon this week, I should esteem if a favour. Yours sincerely, Mary Milne." … Brief … and to the point … at any rate. What sort of a woman is she, Inspector?
HUDSON:	Oh, delightful … Quite the … er … sophisticated type.
SHERWOOD:	M'm …
HUDSON:	She struck me as being rather like that actress … er … Irene Dunne.
SHERWOOD:	(*Rather delighted*) Irene Dunne …? M'm … sounds interesting … (*Re-reading note*) "… and if you can manage to call round and see me one afternoon this week, I should esteem it a favour." M'm … very interesting!

HUDSON laughs.
FADE IN music.

FADE DOWN music.

A door opens.

BUTLER: (*Announcing*) Mr Sherwood, Madam!

LADY MILNE: Thank you, Simpson! Thank you!

The door closes.

LADY MILNE is not at all sophisticated. She is a woman of about fifty-five. Masculine and 'straight to the point.'

SHERWOOD: (*Quietly: obviously surprised*) Lady ... Milne?

LADY MILNE: Ah, Mr Sherwood ... Glad you got my note. Not wasted any time, I see. Good! Sit down ... sit down. Can I get you a drink?

SHERWOOD: Thank you. I think I'd like a whisky and soda.

LADY MILNE: (*Mixing the drink*) Splendid.

SHERWOOD: (*Taking the glass*) Thank you ...

LADY MILNE: You look surprised, Mr Sherwood. (*Amused*) What did you expect ... one of the old Gaiety girls?

SHERWOOD: Er ... not at all, Lady Milne, I merely ...

LADY MILNE: Well, I'm no oil painting. Never have been.

Tiny pause.

SHERWOOD: (*Rather at a loss for words*) Won't you ... er ... join me in a drink?

LADY MILNE: Never touch it. Husband died through cirrhosis of the liver. Put me right off it.

SHERWOOD: Yes, I ... er ... suppose it would.

LADY MILNE: (*After a tiny pause*) I suppose you're wondering why I sent for you?

SHERWOOD: Well, the thought had crossed my mind.

LADY MILNE: You know, Mr Sherwood, I don't know whether you realise it or not, but you've got a pretty shady reputation.

87

SHERWOOD:	Is that why you sent for me, Lady Milne, to tell me …
LADY MILNE:	No! No! No! I sent for you because … (*Suddenly changing her tactics*) Look here, I'll be frank with you, Mr Sherwood. I'm in a mess. A devil of a mess … and I want you to get me out of it.
SHERWOOD:	What makes you think I can?
LADY MILNE:	I don't really know whether you can or not. I'm just hoping. In any case, you're my last chance.
SHERWOOD:	M'm … (*Rather liking her*) Well, supposing … you tell me what it's all about?
LADY MILNE:	Well, as you can probably imagine, I'm on one or two committees. Hospital committees. Charity committees. In fact, to be honest, I'm on so many damn committees I practically have to pass a resolution to get my hair curled. Anyway, to cut a long story short … I'm Chairman of what is known as The International Hospital Fund. They made me Chairman about six months ago. It's a position I've always wanted and … well, I hope that I shall be able to keep it.
SHERWOOD:	What makes you think you won't?
LADY MILNE:	Well, the point is this. You've probably read in the newspapers about this sweepstake we're attempting to organise.
SHERWOOD:	The one that Lord Holborn is opposing?
LADY MILNE:	That's it! Well, the fact of the matter is, they made me Chairman because I promised to make Lord Holborn change

his mind. I felt sure that once I got an interview with the old turkey cock he'd change his tactics. Well, I'm rather afraid he hasn't. In fact, he's just about the most stubborn old bu...zard I've ever come across. I've talked to him, I've written to him, I've even sent the old boy a frantic telegram, but he still carries on with his 'Stop the Sweepstake' campaign. Things are getting serious, Mr Sherwood. Damn serious! If Holborn doesn't change his mind and drop this attitude the sweepstake idea will be finished. The Government are pretty uncertain about it, as it is. (*Emphatically*) And it hasn't got to be finished, Mr Sherwood. The International Hospital Fund needs over eight million pounds, a sweepstake is our only chance. It's got to go through, Mr Sherwood, but the way things are going at the moment, it most certainly won't unless ...

SHERWOOD: Unless Lord Holborn changes his mind and drops his campaign?

LADY MILNE: Exactly.

SHERWOOD: It's all very interesting, Lady Milne, but I don't quite see how precisely Anthony Sherwood fits into the picture?

LADY MILNE: Don't you? Well, I'll be blunt ... I'm offering you ten thousand pounds to make Lord Holborn change his mind.

SHERWOOD: Ten thousand pounds. It's rather a lot of money. I trust it won't come out of The International Hospital Fund?

LADY MILNE: I am personally offering you ten thousand pounds, Mr Sherwood.

SHERWOOD: Oh, well, in that case, Lady Milne, I'll accept five. (*Casually*) Today is the eighteenth. I think you will find that Lord Holborn will have changed his mind by the twenty-second.

FADE IN music.

FADE DOWN music.

CROSS FADE with the sound of a car, it is being driven very swiftly. The car stops. The car door closes. A second door opens.

FADE IN chatter, and a piano being played. It is a typical public house piano.

SHERWOOD: Good evening, Sid …

WILTON: (*Staggered*) Blimey, look whose 'ere … I am glad to see you, Mr Sherwood! What'll you have?

SHERWOOD: Nothing at the moment, Sid … but help yourself and chalk it up.

WILTON: Thanks … I don't mind if I do.

SHERWOOD: I'm looking for Johnny Wayne …

WILTON: Johnny Wayne … did you say? Why, he's upstairs in Room Six. Got a date with a blonde but the blonde don't seem to know anything about it. (*Raising his glass*) Good 'ealth, Mr Sherwood …

SHERWOOD: Thanks. Room Six … you said …?

WILTON: First door on the left … second landing!

SHERWOOD: OK …

FADE background of chatter.

After a pause, a door opens …

SHERWOOD: Hello, Johnny …!

JOHNNY:	(*Softly: amused*) Good … lord! Anthony Sherwood … Why it must be six or seven years since we last …
SHERWOOD:	Six … Six years last August. The Eastbourne job, remember, Johnny?
JOHNNY:	Do I remember? (*Amused*) I never made so much money in my life! You look fit …
SHERWOOD:	I'm all right. And how's the world been treating you?
JOHNNY:	Oh … not too badly … not too badly. (*Suddenly*) Sit down … I'll order some drinks.
SHERWOOD:	Not just at the moment, Johnny. I want to talk …
JOHNNY:	OK …
SHERWOOD:	Have you still got the boys together?
JOHNNY:	Most of them. The gang's pretty much the same … except for Moe. I got rid of Moe … he was too hot headed.
SHERWOOD:	Yes.
Tiny pause.	
JOHNNY:	What is it you want to talk about …?
SHERWOOD:	How would you like to make a thousand, Johnny … for yourself, I mean?
JOHNNY:	(*Laughing*) Chee … what do you think? Anyway, I'd have to cut the boys in, we've got an agreement that …
SHERWOOD:	No. Two hundred each for the boys … The thousand can be quite separate.
JOHNNY:	Phew, that's talking money, we haven't handled L.S.D. like that for years. Say, what do you want us to do, rob the Bank of England?

91

SHERWOOD: Not exactly. It's quite a complicated little
               job, but I've got it worked out for you. The
               only point is, it's urgent ... Damned
               urgent!

JOHNNY: That's all right ... We can start tonight if
               the set up is ok ...

SHERWOOD: Good. Now listen ... and listen carefully!
               There's a retired Judge by the name of
               Lord Holborn. He lives in the country
               about five miles from Guildford. Twelve
               years ago Holborn sentenced a little man
               called Danny O'Hara to a life sentence.
               O'Hara was an Irishman, and judging from
               all accounts, wasn't quite right in the head
               ...

JOHNNY: OK ... go on ...

SHERWOOD: Now, I want you, or one of your men, to
               impersonate this man O'Hara. To break
               into Lord Holborn's house ... to threaten
               the old boy ... Kidnap him, and then take
               him down to the railway line near
               Aldershot Bank. Get him strapped on to
               the line by 7.00 so that the Guildford
               Express ...

JOHNNY: (*Surprised*) Strapped on to the line ...?
               You mean you want us to tie the old boy
               actually ... to ... the ... railway line ... so
               that ... the Guildford Express ...

SHERWOOD: Yes.

JOHNNY: But ... why all this business with the
               railway? If you want us to get rid of the
               guy for you, then ...

SHERWOOD: O'Hara was sentenced for derailing a train, and this is probably the sort of thing he'd do to Holborn if he had the opportunity.

JOHNNY: M'm – what does O'Hara look like?

SHERWOOD: You needn't bother about impersonating him. It's twelve years since Lord Holborn saw Danny O'Hara. Now would, by any chance, the train pull up at …

JOHNNY: You needn't worry about that! The Guildford Express doesn't stop at Aldershot Bank. It never has done … and it never will do!

SHERWOOD: M'm … Well, here's your instructions, Johnny …

FADE IN music.

Slow FADE DOWN.
CROSS FADE with the noise of a train …
The noise of the train is heard for quite a little while … then it FADES to the background and a carriage door is opened. The TICKET COLLECTOR enters …

T. COLLECTOR: Ticket please, sir!

SHERWOOD: Ah, yes, ticket! Now where did … Oh, here we are …

T. COLLECTOR: (*Slowly*) Th..an..k you, sir. (*He clips the ticket*)

SHERWOOD: Are we late?

T. COLLECTOR: No, just about making right time, sir.

SHERWOOD: In that case we should be near Aldershot Bank?

T. COLLECTOR: Yes … only a matter of a minute or two … Look! You can see the beginning of the wood through the window.

SHERWOOD: Oh, yes.

T. COLLECTOR: We don't stop at Aldershot Bank, you know, sir.

SHERWOOD: Is that so?

T. COLLECTOR: Oh, no. There isn't a station. Used to be about twenty odd years ago … pretty little place it was too …

SHERWOOD: Yes, I … suppose it would be.

T. COLLECTOR: (*With a sigh*) Oh, well … I don't suppose I shall be doing this journey again …

SHERWOOD: Really?

T. COLLECTOR: No. Last day … today, sir. I've had thirty-five years of it … enough for my liking.

SHERWOOD: You're retiring …?

T. COLLECTOR: That's right, sir. Starting tomorrow … Putting my feet up … that's all I'm doing from now on.

SHERWOOD: You must have had a pretty exciting time of it, being on the railway that long.

T. COLLECTOR: I don't know that I'd call it exactly exciting, sir.

SHERWOOD: But surely something exciting must have happened every now and again. Someone pulling the communication cord, or …

T. COLLECTOR: (*Interrupting him*) Why, bless my soul! Never known it to happen yet, sir. You don't get people pulling the communication cord … only in books and on the pictures, sir. Why, I've been on this railway thirty-five years an' I've never even seen the … (*Suddenly*) There's Aldershot Bank, sir … about a hundred yards to the right of … (*Staggered*) Blimey, what in 'ell are you doing?

SHERWOOD: (*Politely*) Pulling the communication cord
              … any objection?

T. COLLECTOR: Any … objections!

The train suddenly slows down, and with a tearing of breaks
comes to a standstill … A suitcase falls. Down the corridor
several people scream…
FADE IN music.

Slow FADE DOWN …

JOHNNY WAYNE is in the middle of a fairly long story …

JOHNNY: … Naturally Lord Holborn looked a bit
              bewildered when I came from behind the
              writing desk, and when I started on about
              being   Danny   O'Hara   he   seemed
              completely at sea. Anyway, I didn't stand
              for any nonsense and before the old boy
              could reach for the bell cord I had the
              chloroform pad over his face.

SHERWOOD: Go on. Go on … Johnny …

JOHNNY: Louis and Tony came in through the
              French windows, and before you could say
              … "Jack Robinson" we had him down on
              the   railway   line.   The   effect   of   the
              chloroform had worn off by this time, and
              by jingo, he was certainly excited. When
              the train approached I thought the poor old
              devil was going crazy … anyway, about a
              hundred yards or so away, the train slowed
              down,   and   Frankie   and   Larry   came
              dashing down the slope … all dressed up
              in their glad rags.

SHERWOOD: You mean … dressed as policemen?

JOHNNY: Of   course   …   we   followed   your
              instructions to the letter. They untied the

	old boy, wrapped him up in a blanket, pushed him into a car ... and, well, the rest was plain sailing. Frankie assured him that Danny O'Hara had been caught and Larry dished out your story about Lady Milne.
SHERWOOD:	I hope Larry got the Lady Milne story straight?
JOHNNY:	Oh, he did. He told the old boy that if a certain Lady Milne hadn't pulled the communication cord on the Guildford Express at just the right psychological moment he would have been cut to threads.
SHERWOOD:	(*Amused*) Good.
JOHNNY:	Lord Holborn asked Larry <u>why</u> Lady Milne pulled the communication cord, and Larry said she was on her way back from the races and was so excited at having won so much money, she felt she simply <u>had</u> ... to pull the communication cord.
SHERWOOD:	(*Chuckling*) How did that one go down?
JOHNNY:	According to Frankie the old boy seemed rather bewildered and mumbled something about ... "something good coming out of gambling, after all" ... I'll say one thing for him ... he's a plucky old devil ...
SHERWOOD:	Well, here we are, Johnny ... here's the money I promised you. I haven't crossed the cheque.
JOHNNY:	Thanks.
The door opens.	
NANNY:	Sorry to disturb you, Tony ... only this letter's just arrived ...

SHERWOOD:	That's all right, Nanny ... Johnny's leaving ...
JOHNNY:	All the best ...
SHERWOOD:	(*Lifting his eyes from the letter*) Goodbye, Johnny!

The door closes.

NANNY:	Well, you look pleased with yourself, I must say!
SHERWOOD:	Listen to this, Nanny ... (*Reading*) "Dear Mr Sherwood, A thousand thanks for working the miracle, although I haven't the remotest idea how it happened. The enclosed letter from Lord Holborn arrived this morning, and I am sending it along to you together with the necessary cheque ... yours sincerely, Mary Milne ... P.S. Has the old boy gone crackers?"
NANNY:	From ... Lord Holborn ...?
SHERWOOD:	Let's see what His Lordship says ... (*Reading*) "My dear Lady Milne, ... For certain reasons, which I don't intend to discuss in this letter, I have now definitely decided to abandon my campaign against the proposed sweepstake to be organised by The International Hospital Fund. Since you are Chairman of the organisation it seemed to me only right that you should be the first to learn of my change of attitude. Incidentally, I am happy to hear that you had such a delightful day at the races ..."

SHERWOOD starts chuckling. The buzzer is heard at the main door indicating a new arrival.

NANNY:	Tony, what on earth ...

97

SHERWOOD: (*Amused*) See who that is, Nanny!
A pause. The door opens.
NANNY: It's Inspector Hudson …
HUDSON: Hello, Tony … What's the joke?
SHERWOOD: Hello, Inspector … How are you?
HUDSON: Oh, I'm fine! I just dropped in to see how
              you got along with … er … Lady Milne
              …?
SHERWOOD: You blighter! Quite the … er …
              sophisticated type … Just like Irene Dunne
              …
HUDSON: (*Laughing*) She's a character, isn't she?
SHERWOOD: Absolutely!
HUDSON: Incidentally, I only heard the other day …
              She's Chairman of The International
              Hospital Fund. I hope she wasn't trying to
              get a contribution out of you?
SHERWOOD: It more or less boiled down to that.
              (*Suddenly*) What would you like, Inspector
              …? Whisky and soda …? Brandy …?
HUDSON: Yes, I'd rather like a whisky and soda.
SHERWOOD: Good.
Tiny pause. SHERWOOD is mixing the drinks.
HUDSON: I don't know whether you've seen The
              Evening Standard or not, but they've got
              some sort of a story about Lord Holborn
              dropping his … 'Stop the Sweepstake
              Campaign' … I can hardly believe that.
SHERWOOD: (*Apparently puzzled*) Lord Holborn …?
HUDSON: Yes, don't you remember …? We were
              talking about him the other day …
SHERWOOD: Oh, yes. Yes, of course I remember.
HUDSON: It's funny you know, but I got quite mixed
              up about that old boy. I told you that it was

Lord Holborn who sentenced Danny O'Hara, but it wasn't … It was a judge called Hollingway. I remember it perfectly now because … (*Surprised*) Tony, what is it …? What's the matter …?

But ANTHONY SHERWOOD is laughing … loud and long …
FADE IN music.

END OF EPISODE FOUR

Episode Five
Once Upon A Time

CHARACTERS:

ANTHONY SHERWOOD

MRS DIMBLE (NANNY)

LEWIS MAKEPEACE

EDWARD BIGELOW

PRINCESS INESCOURT

JOHN WYNDHAM

WAITER

CHIEF INSPECTOR HUDSON

Introductory music … Opening announcement …
FADE music

SHERWOOD:	(*Quietly*) You seem to be very engrossed in that book, Nanny.
NANNY:	It isn't a book, dearie, it's a catalogue. (*Suddenly*) Oh, isn't this lovely!
SHERWOOD:	(*Reading*) "Exquisitely picked Russian skins. Full length Sable coat … six hundred guineas…"
NANNY:	Can you imagine me in that? Wouldn't I set the town on fire!
SHERWOOD:	You certainly would!

Tiny pause.

NANNY:	Aren't you going out tonight, Tony?
SHERWOOD:	No. I was going to a party, but I've – er – changed my mind.
NANNY:	(*Anxiously*) Why? Aren't you feeling very well?
SHERWOOD:	Oh, yes, I'm feeling fine. (*Thoughtfully*) "Exquisitely picked Russian skins. Full length Sable coat … Six hundred guineas …" My! Oh, my! You certainly would set the town on fire!

FADE IN music.

FADE DOWN and FADE IN of a tremendous babble of conversation intermingled with laughter. LEWIS MAKEPEACE is attempting, quite unsuccessfully, to make a speech. Suddenly most of the people become aware of this and the conversation dies down.

LEWIS:	Ladies and Gentlemen … or should I say my very good friends … (*Tremendous cheering*) I am very happy that you are all

here with me this evening … on the stage of Her Majesty's Theatre … to celebrate the Four Hundre…th (*He fluffs the word and there is general laughter*) … performance of my play Ladies Love Danger … (*Cheers*). I'm not very good at making speeches but I should like to say how much I appreciate your kindness in coming here this evening … (*Lost for words*) … in … er … coming here this evening … and … well, I hope you all have a very good time.

Cheering … "Good old Lewis!" … "All the best, Lewis!" … "Here's to the next time!" … "Lovely show, my dear!"

In the background a piano is heard … Someone is singing a sophisticated song …

A cocktail glass is knocked off a small table, it falls on to the stage and rolls down to the footlights.

EDWARD: Oh, really … I beg your pardon!

INESCOURT: That's quite all right.

EDWARD: That was certainly mighty clumsy of me. Please let me get you another drink.

EDWARD BIGELOW is a Canadian. He possesses the manner of a self-made man of about forty-five but is nevertheless frequently boyish in a chuckle-headed sort of way.

INESCOURT: (*Pleasantly*) Well, if it's not too much trouble … a Gin and Italian.

EDWARD: (*Delighted*) Why sure! Stay right where you are!

INESCOURT: (*Playfully*) I shan't move an inch! (*After a pause. Softly*) John, who is he?

JOHN: (*Thoughtfully*) I don't know, but did you notice the ring he was wearing?

104

INESCOURT:	(*Amused*) Positively garish!
JOHN:	It's certainly ostentatious, but if the stone is genuine, it must be worth a tidy sum.
INESCOURT:	(*Quietly*) He might be worth knowing …
JOHN:	Who knows? You'll soon find out. (*Casually: moving away*) Give me a ring later.
INESCOURT:	Yes, all right.
Tiny pause.	
EDWARD:	(*Breathless*) Say, I'm sorry to have kept you waiting, it was pretty rough going!
INESCOURT:	(*Laughing*) You've done surprisingly well.
EDWARD:	I only hope that elderly gentleman with the white beard isn't very influential?
INESCOURT:	Why?
EDWARD:	I'm afraid the language I used was rather primitive … more suitable for wide open spaces.
INESCOURT:	Where men are men …?
EDWARD:	(*Laughing*) Yeah, where men are men. (*Suddenly*) Oh, here's your drink. I'm rather afraid I had to get you a sherry.
INESCOURT:	That will do beautifully.
EDWARD:	Well … here's how! (*He drinks*)
INESCOURT:	(*After a pause*) Do you know Lewis very well?
EDWARD:	Lewis? Oh … Makepeace … Oh, yeah, we met about two years ago in California.
INESCOURT:	He's a perfect dear … and most frightfully clever.
EDWARD:	He seems a bright boy. I think this play of his is pretty funny, it certainly made me laugh once or twice.
INESCOURT:	Once or twice? Lewis would be pleased.

EDWARD:	(*Rather boyishly*) Gosh, you're pulling my leg!
INESCOURT:	(*Protestingly*) No, really …
EDWARD:	Say, you know, I think it's about time we introduced ourselves … Kind of got acquainted. The name is Bigelow … Edward Y. Bigelow. Telegraphic address "Lambswool" Toronto …
INESCOURT:	Glad to know you, Mr Bigelow, and I haven't the slightest wish to know what the 'Y' stands for.
EDWARD:	(*Amazed and amused*) Say … you've got a sense of humour, everybody always asks me what the 'Y' stands for.
INESCOURT:	I rather gathered that.
EDWARD:	(*After a tiny pause*) But you haven't told me your name?
INESCOURT:	(*Simply*) Inescourt. Princess Nina Jacqueline Inescourt.
EDWARD:	Princess Inescourt …? Say, no kiddin' …?
INESCOURT:	No kiddin' …
EDWARD:	Er … Russian of course?
INESCOURT:	Of course.
EDWARD:	(*Suddenly embarrassed*) Gosh, I didn't mean to be rude!
INESCOURT:	Don't be silly, you weren't rude, in fact you were really very sweet. Now would you be a dear and reach my wrap for me, it's over near the piano?
EDWARD:	Oh, you're not going?
INESCOURT:	Yes, I'm afraid so. I've had far too many late nights just recently.
EDWARD:	But … let me get you another drink.

INESCOURT:	No. No, I don't think so. Thanks all the same.
EDWARD:	Well ... (*Almost lost for words*) ... Look here, can't we sort of get together some time an' have a kind of evening out or maybe ... (*Suddenly, and with boyish enthusiasm*) Say, Princess, are you interested in jewels ... diamonds, for instance?
INESCOURT:	Why, yes.
EDWARD:	Well, that's my hobby ...
INESCOURT:	(*Amused*) Your ... hobby?
EDWARD:	Collecting 'em, I mean. Just mention the name of Edward Y. Bigelow in Toronto and in the next breath the people say "diamonds." I've got a mighty fine collection. Why don't you drop in one afternoon and give them the once over?
INESCOURT:	(*Laughing*) What can I lose?
EDWARD:	That's swell! I'm staying at The Savoy. Say, how about lunch tomorrow?
INESCOURT:	(*Amused*) You're certainly a pretty fast worker, Mr Bigelow.
EDWARD:	(*Thrilled, yet rather shy*) Gosh, I don't know! What do you say?
INESCOURT:	It's really very sweet of you.
EDWARD:	(*Delighted*) Then that's a date. The Savoy at one ... lunch with Princess Inescourt. (*Proudly*) Chee, way back home that's what they'd call steppin' mighty high ... The Savoy at one ... lunch with Princess Inescourt.

FADE IN music.

FADE DOWN and CROSS FADE with a small restaurant orchestra.

WAITER:	Liqueur, Madam?
INESCOURT:	Er … no thank you.
EDWARD:	Oh, chee … you must have a liqueur! Now what do you say to a crème-de-menthe?
INESCOURT:	(*Laughing*) Oh, very well!
EDWARD:	Crème-de-menthe and a brandy.
WAITER:	Certainly, sir.

A pause.

EDWARD:	Well, what did you think of my little collection?
INESCOURT:	Collection?
EDWARD:	The diamonds.
INESCOURT:	Oh, very nice.
EDWARD:	Very nice! (*Laughing*) Say, Princess, have you got a monopoly in under-statements?
INESCOURT:	(*Amused*) No, seriously, they were really very lovely. What do you intend doing with them?
EDWARD:	(*Puzzled*) Doing with 'em? Why … keeping 'em … Collecting them … it's my hobby.
INESCOURT:	I see.
EDWARD:	Have you ever seen the Peterhoff diamond?
INESCOURT:	The Peterhoff diamond? Why yes, about three years ago … in Paris. (*Puzzled*) Why do you ask?
EDWARD:	(*Casually*) Oh, I just sort of wondered … that's all. Ah, here's the liqueurs!
WAITER:	Crème-de-menthe … Brandy, Monsieur.
EDWARD:	That's fine!

Pause.

INESCOURT:	Why did you mention the Peterhoff diamond?
EDWARD:	Oh, no particular reason.
INESCOURT:	(*After a slight pause*) I see from the newspapers that Mrs Peterhoff is staying at Claridges for a short while.
EDWARD:	At Claridges? …
INESCOURT:	So I believe.

Tiny pause.

EDWARD:	(*Thoughtfully*) That Peterhoff diamond is certainly a mighty fine stone. I'd give my right eye for it. (*Suddenly*) Say, who's this guy coming towards our table, is he a friend of yours?
INESCOURT:	(*Alarmed*) Oh!
SHERWOOD:	(*Suddenly: brightly*) Why, if it isn't Princess Inescourt! This is a delightful surprise. Someone told me that you were in the South of France. Or is the South of France a little too 'hot' for you … this time of year?
INESCOURT:	I haven't been abroad for … quite a little while.
SHERWOOD:	I trust that you are keeping well?
INESCOURT:	Quite well … thank you.
SHERWOOD:	Well, no doubt we shall meet again. (*To EDWARD*) You'll find Princess Inescourt a very 'dear' friend, I assure you. (*He departs*)

Pause.

EDWARD:	(*Puzzled*) Say, who is that …?
INESCOURT:	(*Quietly*) Anthony Sherwood.
EDWARD:	He seems a sarcastic sort of guy.
INESCOURT:	We're not exactly … very good friends.

EDWARD:	(*Amused*) Gosh, I rather gathered that.
INESCOURT:	(*Quietly*) You were talking about the Peterhoff diamond.
EDWARD:	The Peterhoff diamond … Oh, yes …
INESCOURT:	If I remember correctly, you were saying …
EDWARD:	I was saying that I'd give my right eye for it … and by my right eye, I mean … Two hundred thousand dollars.
INESCOURT:	Two hundred thousand dollars … that's a lot of money.
EDWARD:	(*Amused*) Not too much for a miracle worker, and you'd certainly have to be a miracle worker to get the Peterhoff diamond.
INESCOURT:	(*Quietly*) I'm not so sure.
EDWARD:	What do you mean?
INESCOURT:	You provide the two hundred thousand dollars, and I'll provide the miracle.

Tiny pause.

EDWARD:	Are you serious?
INESCOURT:	Quite serious.
EDWARD:	You mean to say that you'd get me the Peterhoff diamond for …
INESCOURT:	(*Quietly*) For … two hundred thousand dollars, Mr Bigelow. Is it a deal?

There is a pause.

| *EDWARD*: | (*Quietly*) Yes. Yes, it's a deal. |

FADE IN music.

FADE DOWN.
JOHN WYNDHAM is speaking …

| JOHN: | (*Irritated*) For heaven's sake, Inescourt, come to your senses. |

INESCOURT:	You think the idea is ridiculous?
JOHN:	Ridiculous? It's completely out of the question! You'd never get the Peterhoff diamond in a thousand years.
INESCOURT:	We shall see.
JOHN:	I've said it before, and I say it again, our best plan is to fleece Bigelow.
INESCOURT:	For what? For ten thousand at the very most … if we get the Peterhoff stone, we're set for life.
JOHN:	If we get it …
INESCOURT:	Why shouldn't we? Mrs Peterhoff is staying at Claridge's. It certainly shouldn't be a very difficult job for one of us to …
JOHN:	Listen, Inescourt! Why do you think the Peterhoff diamond hasn't been touched all these years? Because it's dynamite! There isn't a crook in Europe or on the other side of the Atlantic that dares …
INESCOURT:	The reason the Peterhoff diamond has never been stolen is quite obvious. There isn't a fence in existence that would touch it at even a fifth of its value. So far as we are concerned, however, that difficulty doesn't arise. Bigelow has promised us two hundred thousand dollars, that's a certainty. Now if … (*A door opens*) What is it, Marion?
MARION:	The evening paper, Madam, and two letters which arrived by the afternoon post.
INESCOURT:	Put them on the desk.
MARION:	Yes, Madam. (*The door closes*)
INESCOURT:	… Apart from anything else, there's absolutely no risk … so far as Bigelow is

	concerned. It's not like passing the stone on to a fence for re-cutting.
JOHN:	But what the devil does he want it for?
INESCOURT:	Oh, he's crazy on diamonds. You should see his collection.

The telephone commences to ring.

JOHN:	It's all right, I'll take it. (*Lifts receiver*) Hello? ... Yes ... Oh, it's you, Cary ... What's the matter, you sound pretty excited? ... What news? (*Puzzled*) ...No, we've got a copy here but we haven't had a chance to ... (*Suddenly*) What? (*Amazed*) Cary ... is ... this ... true? ... Yes, yes, of course, if it's in the papers ... Yes ... All right ... Thanks for ringing. (*Replaces the receiver*)
INESCOURT:	What is it? ...
JOHN:	Where's the evening paper?
INESCOURT:	It's on the desk. John ... what's the matter?
JOHN:	I'm afraid we're too late. The Peterhoff diamond was stolen at three-thirty this afternoon.
INESCOURT:	But – but surely ... that can't be true!
JOHN:	We'll soon find out, it's supposed to be in the paper. (*He opens the evening paper*)

Pause.

JOHN:	It's true all right.
INESCOURT:	(*Excitedly*) Here ... let me see.
JOHN:	Cary was laughing like mad. He thought it was a huge joke. He said there wasn't a fence in Europe who would touch it.
INESCOURT:	He's about right, too. (*Suddenly*) John, we've got to find out who pulled this job

112

	and make him an offer … at all cost we've got to get the diamond.
JOHN:	Yes … if we could once get hold of the fool, I reckon we'd get it for ten thousand … twenty at the most … and then we could pass it on to Bigelow. (*Thoughtfully*) Who would pull a job like this …?
INESCOURT:	(*Quietly*) I don't know …
JOHN:	It says in the newspaper that the police have got some sort of a clue.
INESCOURT:	That doesn't help us any.
JOHN:	(*Quietly*) I'm not so sure.
INESCOURT:	What do you mean?
JOHN:	(*Thoughtfully*) What's Claridge's number? Oh, I remember … (*He dials*)

Tiny pause.

JOHN:	Hello? Claridges …? Would you be good enough to put me through to Mrs Peterhoff, please? This is Inspector … er … Jackson of Scotland Yard … Thank you.
INESCOURT:	What on earth …
JOHN:	Sh! (*Suddenly*) Mrs Peterhoff? … Inspector Jackson speaking of Scotland Yard … I'm very sorry to trouble you, Madam, but I am wondering if you would be good enough to repeat certain facts which you have already placed at our disposal … It's simply a question of … Yes, that's right, Madam … No, I simply wanted to know the names of any visitors you may have received during the course of the day … Yes, that's right … A Miss Spencer …? Yes … Dr Hartman … Is he

113

	the hotel doctor? … Oh, I see … Yes … A Mr Huxley … Yes … Had you met Mr Huxley before? … Oh, yes … I understand … (*Amazed*) Who? … What time was that…? Yes … Yes, thank you. (*Replaces the receiver*) Well, I'm damned!
INESCOURT:	(*Alarmed*) What is it?
JOHN:	I know the man the police suspect, and by George, I reckon they're right!
INESCOURT:	Who is it?
JOHN:	(*Quietly*) Anthony Sherwood …
INESCOURT:	Anthony Sherwood …!
JOHN:	The Prince of Rogues …

FADE IN music.

FADE DOWN of music.
ANTHONY SHERWOOD is finishing his breakfast.

SHERWOOD:	I should like another cup of the dark, luke-warm liquid you choose to call coffee, Mrs Dimble.
NANNY:	It's the best coffee you've ever tasted, my lad, or even likely to taste, if you ask me.
SHERWOOD:	Did anyone ring up while I was out last night?
NANNY:	I don't know, I went to the pictures.
SHERWOOD:	You always seem to be going to the pictures these days. They'll be having you on the screen next.
NANNY:	(*Laughing*) Coo, that'll be the day! It'll be goodbye to Myrna what's-er-name when I get going!

The telephone rings.

SHERWOOD:	(*Amused*) It's all right, Nanny, I'll take it. (*Lifts receiver*) Hello? … Yes … Who? …

	Oh, yes, send her straight up … Thank you. (*Replaces the receiver*) Never mind about the coffee, Nanny, and you can take the tray.
NANNY:	You haven't finished your breakfast!
SHERWOOD:	It's all right, Nanny, now don't fuss … (*Thoughtfully*) Nine-thirty … M'm – She hasn't lost much time …
NANNY:	I go to the trouble of cooking a perfectly lovely breakfast 'an all you …

FADE voice.
A door closes.
Tiny pause.
A bell rings. A second door opens.

SHERWOOD:	Why Princess Inescourt, this is a pleasant surprise! And dropping in at breakfast time too, how frightfully original!
INESCOURT:	Sherwood, I want to see you about something rather urgent, and I haven't much time at my disposal.
SHERWOOD:	Come inside, Princess! Come inside! I trust you'll forgive my somewhat dishevelled appearance.

The door closes.
There is a pause.

INESCOURT:	You know, Tony, I always thought you were a bit of a fool but now I'm quite certain.
SHERWOOD:	M'm – an interesting observation. What makes you so certain?
INESCOURT:	(*Quietly*) The Peterhoff diamond.
SHERWOOD:	The Peterhoff diamond? (*Tiny pause*) I don't understand.
INESCOURT:	Don't you?

Slight pause.

SHERWOOD: (*Suddenly amused*) Good heavens, you don't think that I, by any chance, was responsible for the disappearance of the …

INESCOURT: Yes, Tony, the thought had crossed my mind.

SHERWOOD: But that's ridiculous!

INESCOURT: Why ridiculous? You paid Mrs Peterhoff a visit yesterday afternoon.

SHERWOOD: My! Oh, my! News does travel!

INESCOURT: What on earth you hope to get out of the Peterhoff diamond, goodness only knows! There certainly isn't a fence in Europe that would touch it.

SHERWOOD: You seem to be pretty well informed.

INESCOURT: I know what I'm talking about when it comes to diamonds, especially if they happen to be 'hot'.

SHERWOOD: Well, what would you say the Peterhoff diamond was worth?

INESCOURT: Eight or ten thousand, certainly no more.

SHERWOOD: (*Amused*) Eight or ten … You're crazy! If it's worth a penny it's worth the best part of forty thousand.

INESCOURT: (*Quietly*) Tony, the diamond itself may be worth forty thousand, as a matter of fact I think it's probably worth considerably more. But the point is …

SHERWOOD: The point is … you want the Peterhoff diamond, don't you?

INESCOURT: Yes … and I'm prepared to pay ten thousand for it. Not a penny more.

SHERWOOD: (*After a slight pause*) I'll be quite frank with you, I want to get rid of it. But ten thousand is hardly …

INESCOURT: Ten thousand is a great deal more than you'd get from anyone else, and you know it.

SHERWOOD: I'm not so sure. After all, you must have something in mind, Princess. You obviously aren't going to wear the diamond yourself.

INESCOURT: (*Determined*) I'm offering you ten thousand, Sherwood … Take it or leave it!

Tiny pause.

SHERWOOD: Would you care for a cup of coffee, Princess, before we leave for the bank?

INESCOURT: Does that mean …?

SHERWOOD: It means you get the diamond, and I get the ten thousand … cash!

FADE IN music.

FADE DOWN.

A door opens.

NANNY: (*Anxiously*) So here you are at last! My word you have been a time, Tony. (*Softly*) Inspector Hudson's here … he's been waiting about ten minutes.

SHERWOOD: (*Softly*) OK … (*Brightly*) Why, if it isn't old Sherlock Holmes himself …

HUDSON: Hello, Tony!

SHERWOOD: Sorry to have kept you waiting. (*Taking off his overcoat*) Brr! Quite chilly out …

HUDSON: (*Softly*) Tony …

SHERWOOD: Yes? (*Tiny pause*) My word, you do look serious!

117

HUDSON:	(*Quietly*) I've got a warrant out, Tony.
SHERWOOD:	A warrant ...? What for?
HUDSON:	You know perfectly well what for ...
SHERWOOD:	(*Amused*) You don't mean for my arrest?
HUDSON:	Yes. (*Officially*) I must warn you that anything you may say may be taken ...
SHERWOOD:	(*Laughing*) Oh, Inspector! Inspector, please!
HUDSON:	This isn't a laughing matter. I'm serious. Damn serious!
SHERWOOD:	(*Bewildered*) But what's it all about? I don't understand ...?
HUDSON:	(*Slightly annoyed*) Don't you? Permit me to refresh your memory. Yesterday afternoon you paid a visit to a Mrs Peterhoff at Claridge's Hotel. That was at three-thirty. At four o'clock precisely Mrs Peterhoff reported to Scotland Yard that the famous Peterhoff diamond had been stolen. Stolen by someone who had had the audacity to ...
SHERWOOD:	One moment! One moment, Inspector ... please! In the first place I did visit Claridge's hotel yesterday afternoon for the very good reason, to renew an acquaintanceship which I had made in New York several years ago with – take a grip on yourself, Inspector – Mrs Peterhoff. I'd read in the newspapers that Mrs Peterhoff was staying at Claridge's and I went along to pay my respects. But when I arrived at the hotel a rather extraordinary thing happened.
HUDSON:	What do you mean?

SHERWOOD: Well, I discovered that the Mrs Peterhoff staying at Claridge's was not the real Mrs Peterhoff at all, but simply an imposter.

HUDSON: An imposter? But – that's ridiculous!

SHERWOOD: Oh, no it isn't. In fact it's far from being ridiculous. Take a look at this cable, it's in answer to a cable I sent to the real Mrs Peterhoff at Palm Beach, Florida. It arrived early this morning.

Tiny pause.

HUDSON: (*Reading*) "Story quite fantastic. Stop. Peterhoff diamond at present at Chases Bank, New York. Stop. Inform Scotland Yard. Ena Peterhoff." (*After a slight pause*) M'm – this … this sounds genuine enough.

SHERWOOD: Oh, it's genuine all right.

HUDSON: (*Bewildered*) Then why the devil did this woman at Claridge's …

The telephone rings.

SHERWOOD: Excuse me. (*Lifts the receiver*) Hello? … Yes … Pardon? … Oh just hold the line one moment, please. (*To HUDSON*) It's for you, Inspector.

HUDSON: Oh. (*Takes the receiver*) Hello? … Oh, good morning, Sir … Yes? … Well, I'm not surprised to be quite honest, Sir … Apparently Sherwood realised that the woman at Claridge's was … (*Amused*) Well, I'm afraid we'll have to, Sir … Yes, that would be best … Thank you, Sir. (*He rings off*)

SHERWOOD: Well?

HUDSON:	(*Quietly*) That was the Assistant Commissioner. You were quite right, Tony. They've had a cable from Mrs Peterhoff … the real Mrs Peterhoff. The diamond apparently is in New York … in Chases Bank.
SHERWOOD:	And the young lady at Claridge's?
HUDSON:	So far as I can make out she seems to have completely disappeared. (*Thoughtfully*) I wonder what the devil she was up to? She can't have got anything out of it!
SHERWOOD:	Probably some sort of a hoax.
HUDSON:	M'm, obviously … I should say. Oh, well … I must be off!
SHERWOOD:	(*Amused*) Do drop in again, George, especially when you've got a warrant out for me. I love that bit about … "anything you may say will be taken down and used" … (*He chuckles*)
HUDSON:	One of these days you'll laugh once too often, Tony!

FADE chuckles.
A door opens and closes.
Pause.

NANNY:	Good gracious me, I thought he was never going!
SHERWOOD:	(*Amused*) I could see your ears positively flapping against the keyhole, Nanny!
NANNY:	Oh, that's not true! (*Quietly*) What's that you've got in your pocket, Tony?
SHERWOOD:	Just a present from Princess Inescourt. Ten thousand pounds …
NANNY:	Ten … (*Amazed*) But … what for?

SHERWOOD:	A very poor copy of the Peterhoff diamond.
NANNY:	But … does … she know it's a copy?
SHERWOOD:	No, I'm afraid she doesn't, Nanny.
NANNY:	(*Bewildered*) Oh, Tony … what's this all about? First of all I read that the Peterhoff diamond is missing. Then I overhear you tell Inspector Hudson that …
SHERWOOD:	(*Amused*) You do seem perplexed, Mrs Dimble!
NANNY:	I don't know whether I'm standing on my head or my heels …
SHERWOOD:	Well, once upon a time, Nanny, there was an unscrupulous young lady who lived by her wits, and her name was Princess Inescourt. One evening, when the Princess had very little to do, she went to a party. Now it so happened that at this party there was a young man who called himself Edward Bigelow, which was a really naughty thing to do since his name was not Bigelow, and by a strange set of circumstances he was not christened Edward. Indeed, he bore the somewhat unromantic label of … Jonathan White. Now Jonathan White, alias Edward Bigelow, strikes up an acquaintance with the Princess and professes an interest in a certain valuable stone known to the world at large as the Peterhoff diamond. In order to add the Peterhoff diamond to his already apparently priceless collection Mr Bigelow informs the Princess that he is quite prepared to pay not less than sixty

thousand pounds. The Princess is intrigued. She has already read in the newspapers, as Anthony Sherwood thoroughly intended that she should do so, that Mrs Peterhoff is staying at Claridge's, and since the Princess is a woman of experience she sees no reason why Mrs Peterhoff shouldn't very quickly part with the Peterhoff diamond. But it is not the real Mrs Peterhoff staying at Claridge's but a friend of Anthony Sherwood's by the name of Madeline Kent. And as soon as Miss Kent hears from Mr Bigelow to the effect that the Princess is on the war path, she immediately contacts Scotland Yard and the newspapers with the story that the diamond has been stolen, at the same time taking great care to throw suspicion on to Anthony Sherwood. Sooner or later the Princess hears about Anthony Sherwood visiting Claridge's and quite naturally – as was intended from the very beginning – jumps to the conclusion that he is the possessor of the Peterhoff diamond. Result? She offers ten thousand pounds for what is nothing more nor less than a third-rate copy. Meanwhile of course, Mr Edward Bigelow, alias Jonathan White, and our dear friend Madeline Kent retire to the country to … er … await their share of the … er … proceeds.

NANNY: (*Staggered*) Well … what ever will you think of next …?

SHERWOOD: (*Amused*) Here we are, Nanny …

122

NANNY: (*Amazed*) What's this …? Seven hundred
              pounds! But – but what's this for?
SHERWOOD: Because I'm rather afraid there's a moral
              to the story.
NANNY: A moral …?
SHERWOOD: Yes. (*Tiny pause*) Never let your
              housekeeper take a liking to Sable …

And Anthony Sherwood laughs.

END OF EPISODE FIVE

Episode Six
Watch Your Step, Mr Sherwood!

CHARACTERS:

ANTHONY SHERWOOD

MRS DIMBLE (NANNY)

BENNY

SIMS

INSPECTOR WILLIAMS

CHIEF INSPECTOR BAILEY

CHIEF INSPECTOR HUDSON

REPORTER

TOMMY DEACON

JOHN WYNDHAM

PRINCESS INESCOURT

MR METRO (a Pekinese)

Introductory music … Opening announcement …
FADE music.

BENNY: (*Softly*) You're taking a devil of a time!
SIMS: It's this second dial … I can't get the
                    combination straight! … (*Suddenly*) Mind
                    that wire!!!
In the background a bell is heard.
BENNY: My God, that's the alarm …
SIMS: (*Desperately*) Listen!
Voices are heard.
BENNY: It's the night watchman … he's coming up
                    here!
SIMS: (*Excitedly*) I've got the safe open … We
                    can't leave now, not without …
BENNY: Get down!!! Here he comes!!!
The door opens.
NIGHT WATCHMAN: Hello … What's going on here?
SIMS: Let him have it!
FADE IN of revolver shots.
FADE IN of music.

*FADE DOWN, and CROSS FADE with the sound of a fast
approaching car. The car stops. A door slams.*
WILLIAMS: (*With authority*) Rogers, Thomson and
                    Hurst take the main entrance! Smith and
                    Mitchell take the two sides! Now be
                    careful … We don't want any slip-ups.
                    Sherwood isn't a fool, remember …
FADE IN music.

CROSS FADE with dance orchestra and people dancing.
SHERWOOD: Tired of dancing, Nanny?

127

NANNY:	(*Exhausted*) I think I'd like to sit down, Tony. I'm feeling rather hot and bothered …
SHERWOOD:	(*Laughing*) I thought you looked rather exhausted.

Tiny pause.

WAITER:	Mr Sherwood …?
SHERWOOD:	Yes.
WAITER:	There's a gentleman to see you, sir … He's waiting in the vestibule …
SHERWOOD:	(*After a slight hesitation*) Yes, all right … I shan't be a second, Nanny.

FADE dance orchestra to the background.

A door opens.

WILLIAMS:	Mr Sherwood … Anthony Sherwood?
SHERWOOD:	Yes.
WILLIAMS:	My name is Williams. Divisional-Inspector Williams of the Criminal …
SHERWOOD:	(*Pleasantly*) Why Inspector, this is a pleasure!
WILLIAMS:	I must warn you that anything you may say will be taken down and …
SHERWOOD:	(*Amused*) Say … what is this?
WILLIAMS:	(*Grimly: rather delighted*) Mr Sherwood … you're under arrest!!!

QUICK FADE in of music.

FADE DOWN.

CHIEF INSPECTOR BAILEY is speaking. He is rather abrupt in manner.

BAILEY:	Mr Sherwood, there seems very little point in beating about the bush. The position, as far as we are concerned, is quite clear. Last night, between the hours of nine and

128

twelve fifteen, a robbery took place at Rudolf Haimer's, the jewellers, in Hatton Garden. A necklace was stolen ... rather a valuable necklace ... but apart from that interesting detail the night watchman was murdered. Now, murder, my dear Mr Sherwood ...

SHERWOOD: (*Interrupting*) Murder, my dear Chief-Inspector Bailey, is not my line of business, you know that as well as I do.

BAILEY: Then you deny having ... er ... murdered the night watchman?

SHERWOOD: (*Rather annoyed*) Deny it? I even deny having been near Rudolf Haimer's last night, or any other night for that matter!!!

BAILEY: Then how do you account for the fact that a fingerprint ... a fingerprint from your left hand, Mr Sherwood ... was found on the safe?

SHERWOOD: (*Amazed*) My ... finger ... print ... on the safe? You're joking ...

BAILEY: It's hardly my idea of a joke, although honesty compels me to admit that a sense of ...

The door opens.

HUDSON: Sorry to trouble you, Bailey, but this report ... (*Surprised*) Hello, Tony ... What's going on here ...?

SHERWOOD: You'd better ask the Inspector, he seems to know all the answers.

HUDSON: What's happened?

BAILEY: We found Sherwood's fingerprint on the safe at Haimer's.

129

HUDSON:	What!!! (*Laughing*) Oh, but that's preposterous …
BAILEY:	I'm glad you think so. Anyway, there's a copy of the report, together with the fingerprints.

Tiny pause.

SHERWOOD:	(*Puzzled*) Hudson … What is it?
HUDSON:	(*Quietly*) My God, there's no doubt about it. The prints are exactly the same.
SHERWOOD:	But damn it man …
HUDSON:	Sherwood didn't go near Haimer's last night … he couldn't have done so.
BAILEY:	What makes you so certain?
HUDSON:	I called for him shortly before seven, and we went straight to Lord Maxtons … we were there until twenty past two this morning.
BAILEY:	(*Staggered*) Is … this … true, Sherwood?
SHERWOOD:	Why, yes, of course …
BAILEY:	Well … I'm … damned!!!

FADE IN of music.

FADE DOWN of the sudden smashing of glass. A police whistle is heard. General revolver shots. A car makes a very speedy departure.
FADE IN of a telephone ringing.

FADE DOWN.

REPORTER:	(*Excited on phone*) Give me the city desk … Jump to it … Hello, is that you, Regan? Morgan here … All set? OK … (*Dictating*) Twenty-four hours after sensational Park Lane robbery, Scotland Yard arrests Anthony Sherwood, the

Prince of Rogues ... (*Chuckling*) Yes ...
Anthony Sherwood ... isn't it a "pip"...?

QUICK FADE up of music.

FADE DOWN.

SHERWOOD: This is the second time that you've
brought me to Scotland Yard in a week,
Inspector, I trust that this time you have
something a little more concrete than ...

BAILEY: Believe me, Sherwood, we shan't detain
you any longer than is necessary ...

HUDSON: (*Quietly*) Tony, did you have anything to
do with this business in Park Lane?

SHERWOOD: Park Lane? (*Slightly amused*) You don't
mean the Curzon Street robbery about ...

HUDSON: Yes.

SHERWOOD: Why, good lord, no!

BAILEY: Where were you on Tuesday night ...?

SHERWOOD: On Tuesday night? I was at Bramley
Lodge, near Evesham ... Paul Temple's
place. I stayed the night.

BAILEY: (*Quietly: amazed*) Was ... Temple ...
there?

SHERWOOD: Why, yes, of course ... (*Suddenly*) I say,
what is all this ...?

HUDSON: (*Quietly*) A glass panel was smashed on
the Curzon Street job, it led into the
showroom at the back of the premises. On
the panel, Tony ... we found your
fingerprint.

SHERWOOD: (*Amazed*) My fingerprint ... but ... that's
impossible!

HUDSON:	No … it's your fingerprint all right. I've checked it and double checked it … there's not the slightest doubt …
BAILEY:	There wasn't the slightest doubt when we found his print at Haimers, but he had an alibi.
SHERWOOD:	It isn't a question of having an alibi, Inspector, it's simply a question of stating the truth. The night the Haimer robbery took place I was at Lord Maxton's …
BAILEY:	Yes … yes … yes, we've checked up on that …
SHERWOOD:	Last Tuesday, the night of the Curzon Street robbery … I was at Evesham … You can check up on that also …
BAILEY:	I'm damned if I can make head or tail of this! There's not the slightest doubt about it being your fingerprint …
SHERWOOD:	Not the slightest doubt …
BAILEY:	… and yet on each occasion you've had an absolutely fool-proof alibi. (*Bewildered*) It's utterly and completely beyond me …
SHERWOOD:	It seems to me, Inspector, that, on both occasions, I've been rather lucky. It would have been rather awkward for me, wouldn't it, if I couldn't have explained my movements on … say … last Tuesday evening?
HUDSON:	Extremely awkward.
BAILEY:	If you take my advice … you'll watch your step, Mr Sherwood!

FADE IN music.

Slow FADE DOWN.

SHERWOOD: (*Rather impatiently*) What time is it,
                 Nanny?
NANNY: That clock's right, Tony, I told you that
                 five minutes ago …
SHERWOOD: No one rang up while I was out?
NANNY: No, dearie … no one rang up while you
                 were out …
The flat bell is heard.
SHERWOOD: (*Quickly*) That's the door, Nanny …
                 quickly …
NANNY: All right … All right, Tony …
Pause.
A door opens. TOMMY DEACON enters.
SHERWOOD: (*Delighted*) Hello, Tommy …
TOMMY: Sorry I'm late. It's a devil of a job getting
                 here.
SHERWOOD: That's all right … take your things off,
                 Tommy …
TOMMY: (*Shivering*) Brr … pretty chilly out
                 tonight.
SHERWOOD: Help yourself to a drink …
TOMMY: Thanks. (*He does so*)
Slight pause.
SHERWOOD: Well, did you find out … what I wanted to
                 know …?
TOMMY: I did …
SHERWOOD: Good!
TOMMY: I was wrong about the Soho gang, Tony,
                 they'd nothing to do with either the Park
                 Lane spot o' bother or the Rudolf Haimer
                 job … both jobs were pulled by an entirely
                 new outfit …
SHERWOOD: Who's behind them, do you know?

133

TOMMY:	Well, I've heard a rumour that it's a woman called Princess Inescourt, but whether …
SHERWOOD:	Princess Inescourt? Then that accounts for it … No wonder they're trying to frame me.
TOMMY:	Do you know her?
SHERWOOD:	Yes, I know the young lady all right …
TOMMY:	Well, she's certainly smart.
SHERWOOD:	They don't make them any smarter, Tommy, believe me.
TOMMY:	I tell you what I did find out, although it took me a devil of a time to do so … I found out how she was working this fingerprint idea …
SHERWOOD:	How?
TOMMY:	Well, I was talking to an American called Stoneburg, and he was telling me it is possible to take an exact copy of a fingerprint and by means of a gelatine setting have a sort of stamp made … It's not a very easy thing to do, but nevertheless it's certainly well within the bounds of possibility.
SHERWOOD:	(*Thoughtfully*) Yes, that's what she's been doing all right …
TOMMY:	The point is, while she's got the stamp, you've got to watch yourself … otherwise you'll be framed …
SHERWOOD:	(*Quietly*) Yes …
TOMMY:	Do you mind if I have another drink?
SHERWOOD:	No, of course not … go ahead.
TOMMY:	Thanks. (*He mixes a drink*)

Tiny pause.

SHERWOOD:	I suppose you've heard about Simons …?
TOMMY:	You mean J.J. Simons … the man with the Nurembourg collection …?
SHERWOOD:	Yes.
TOMMY:	I heard that he was staying in town … at the Grand, isn't he?
SHERWOOD:	So I believe.
TOMMY:	Not a very nice customer, judging from all accounts.
SHERWOOD:	Nevertheless, that collection of his must be worth a pretty penny.
TOMMY:	I know where I could get fifteen thousand for the pendant alone.
SHERWOOD:	That's interesting, Tommy.
TOMMY:	(*Amused*) It's certainly a proposition.
SHERWOOD:	(*After a slight pause*) You don't happen to know where Princess Inescourt is staying at the moment …?
TOMMY:	Well, I did hear a rumour that she was staying at Claridge's under the name of Lady Westmoreland, but whether it's true or not I don't know. She's rather a difficult sort of person to keep track of …
SHERWOOD:	(*Thoughtfully*) Yes. (*Suddenly*) Tommy … you say that you could get fifteen thousand for the pendant … the pendant from the Nurembourg collection?
TOMMY:	Yes. But it's no good thinking on that, Tony. You'd need a fool proof alibi to pull a job like that …
SHERWOOD:	Maybe Princess Inescourt … could … provide me with one …
TOMMY:	(*Puzzled*) What do you mean …? I don't understand …?

SHERWOOD: (*Amused*) Don't you, Tommy …? Don't
              … you …?

FADE IN music.

*CROSS FADE with a dance orchestra. It stops. There is the
background of chatter. The orchestra continues.*

JOHN: There's no doubt about it, Sherwood's
              been lucky … damn lucky … If he hadn't
              produced a really first-class alibi on both
              occasions he'd have been caught … and
              caught pretty badly too.

INESCOURT: Don't worry, John, we'll get him all right.
              That fingerprint idea was a brain wave.

JOHN: You're not thinking of using it on the
              Carlton Bank job, by any chance?

INESCOURT: Yes. If we can get Sherwood framed for
              robbing the Carlton bank he'll be out of
              circulation for a long time to come.

JOHN: I'm not too happy about this Carlton
              business, Inescourt. There's one or two
              points which don't seem to me to be really
              convincing. I mean a bank job isn't
              exactly …

INESCOURT: (*Interrupting him*) We can't talk here,
              John, let's go up to my room …

JOHN: Yes … all right. (*Turning from the table*)
              Waiter! My bill … please!

FADE UP dance orchestra.

FADE DOWN.
*A door opens. A small Pekinese dog starts to bark rather
enthusiastically.*

JOHN: Hello! Mr Metro seems rather excited …

136

INESCOURT:	(*Speaking to the dog*) What is it, darling? Is the poor little doggie hungry? Would the darling little itsy … bitsy like a biscuit …? (*Taking the Pekinese in her arms*) That's a sweet little pet …
JOHN:	(*Laughing*) You seem to think more of that dog than … (*He stops talking rather suddenly*)
INESCOURT:	What's the matter?
JOHN:	(*Quietly*) Someone's been in here! Look at the desk …
INESCOURT:	(*Alarmed*) John … it's been forced!
JOHN:	Yes. (*There is a pause. The desk is opened*) What's missing?
INESCOURT:	(*Softly*) Nothing … so far as I can see. There was a cheque for twenty pounds, but … Oh, that's all right … (*Suddenly*) John! John! They've taken the gelatine stamp … Sherwood's fingerprint stamp … It was here … In this box …
JOHN:	(*Alarmed*) My God! Are you sure?
INESCOURT:	Yes.
JOHN:	(*Thoughtfully*) Inescourt … you don't think … Anthony Sherwood's been here …?
INESCOURT:	(*Quietly*) I don't know … I don't know …
FADE IN music.	

FADE DOWN.

REPORTER:	(*On telephone*) Be quick with that number, Miss … It's urgent! (*Tiny pause*) Hello? … Hello? (*Suddenly*) Is that you, Regan? … Morgan here … (*Chuckling*) Oh, Mister Regan, have I got a story!!! … M'm …

What's happened …? Boy, what hasn't happened!!! Somebody's pinched the Nurembourg pendant … How was it done? Don't ask me, Regan … I only find the news … I don't make it!!! … Yes … Yes … OK …

FADE IN music.

FADE DOWN.

SHERWOOD: Now you've got your instructions, Nanny.

NANNY: (*Rather bewildered*) Yes, but I don't understand, Tony. Why should …

SHERWOOD: It's really quite simple, Nanny. When Tommy Deacon arrives with the Pekinese, I want you to take the dog into the kitchen. Later, when Inspector Hudson arrives on the scene, let the dog go free so that …

The flat bell is heard.

SHERWOOD: There's Tommy … Jump to it. Nanny!

The door opens. TOMMY enters carrying the Pekinese.

TOMMY: I've had a game with this damn thing, I can tell you …

The dog barks.

SHERWOOD: Take the dog, Nanny … It's all right, it won't bite you …

NANNY: I'm not so sure, my lad!

NANNY leaves.

SHERWOOD: (*Anxiously*) Well, what happened?

TOMMY: Oh, everything went beautifully … (*Taking off his overcoat*) Here's your coat and scarf …

SHERWOOD: Thanks. You didn't forget to use the fingerprint stamp?

TOMMY: No.

SHERWOOD:	What time was it Tommy when you left …?
TOMMY:	About ten past eleven.
SHERWOOD:	Good. Did anyone see you?
TOMMY:	Only the lift boy and he only caught a glimpse of me … Here, you'd better take this stamp, Tony.
SHERWOOD:	Oh, thanks.
TOMMY:	You got away with the Nurembourg job then …?
SHERWOOD:	Yes. It was really easier than I expected. Your friend Zanovitch called about an hour ago, he said that with a bit of luck he might get twenty thousand for the pendant.
TOMMY:	He did? Good …

The flat bell is heard.

TOMMY:	Hello … Who's that?
SHERWOOD:	(*Quietly*) Probably Hudson … You'd better let yourself out through the library … You know the way.
TOMMY:	Sure. I'll see you later, Tony.
SHERWOOD:	Yes, most likely Thursday …
TOMMY:	Good!

He leaves.

A pause.

The door opens.

SHERWOOD:	(*Pleasantly*) Hello, Inspector!
HUDSON:	(*Quietly*) Hello, Tony … Alone?
SHERWOOD:	Why yes, of course … except for Mrs Dimble.
HUDSON:	M'm …
SHERWOOD:	Can I get you a drink?
HUDSON:	No, thanks … (*Tiny pause*) Tony … You know why I'm here … Don't you?

139

SHERWOOD:	No … I haven't the faintest idea. (*After a slight pause*) Is anything the matter?
HUDSON:	Where were you last night?
SHERWOOD:	Last night? Oh, just out … and … about.
HUDSON:	Yes … but where?
SHERWOOD:	I say, what is all this?
HUDSON:	I've – I've got a warrant out for your arrest.
SHERWOOD:	(*Amused*) Well, you needn't look so grim about it. It's not the first time … and ten to one it won't be the last.
HUDSON:	Yes, but … (*Rather more friendly*) … Well, I'm damned if I can make head or tail of it, Tony. A woman called Lady Westmoreland reported that her Pekinese dog had been stolen … We sent Williams down to Claridge's to investigate and he came back with the story that a man had been seen leaving the hotel at ten past eleven who was obviously Anthony Sherwood … or Anthony Sherwood's double. Anyway, to cut a long story short, we searched the apartment and damn me if we didn't find your fingerprint on the writing desk.
SHERWOOD:	On the writing desk …? But what does that prove …?
HUDSON:	Well, it proves that you must have been in the apartment, doesn't it? Unless, of course, you've got a foolproof alibi.
SHERWOOD:	Now, I ask you, Inspector, what on earth would I want with a Pekinese …?
HUDSON:	That's exactly what I said to Bailey!
SHERWOOD:	(*Chuckling*) A Pekinese!

HUDSON: (*Chuckling also*) Dam' silly!!! (*Suddenly*)
                   Hello, what's that?

In the background the dog can be heard barking.

SHERWOOD: I never heard anything …

HUDSON: I could have sworn that I …

*The door opens and the Pekinese dashes into the room
followed by Mrs Dimble.*

NANNY: Come here! Come here! Come here … you
                   little devil!!! I'll teach you to …
                   (*Suddenly*) Oh, I beg your pardon, sir …

HUDSON: (*Staggered*) Why, it's … the …
                   Pekinese!!! (*Bewildered*) What on earth …

SHERWOOD: (*Quietly*) All right, Nanny …

NANNY: Be quiet … you naughty dog!

The door closes.

SHERWOOD: Well, I'll need a pretty good lawyer to get
                   me out of this mess, won't I?

HUDSON: Tony … why on earth did you go to the
                   trouble to steal a perfectly harmless …

The telephone interrupts him.

SHERWOOD: Just a minute, George. (*Lifts receiver*)
                   Hello? … Who? … Oh yes … Hold the
                   line … It's for you, Inspector.

HUDSON: (*Taking receiver*) Thanks. (*On the phone*)
                   Hello? … Oh, hello Bailey … M'm …
                   (*Staggered*) What!!! … When did that
                   happen? … Ten past eleven … Good lord!
                   … Yes, I'll get straight back … Yes, of
                   course! (*Replaces receiver*)

SHERWOOD: What's happened?

HUDSON: What's happened! You seem to be
                   slipping, Tony. At precisely the same time
                   that you confiscated a Pekinese someone

141

	calmly marches away with the Nurembourg collection.
SHERWOOD:	No!!!
HUDSON:	Yes!!!
SHERWOOD:	The Nurembourg collection! Why, Inspector … the pendant alone must be worth ten thousand …
HUDSON:	Twenty!
SHERWOOD:	Twenty … You don't say!!!
HUDSON:	Absolutely … (*Chuckling*) You know, Tony, I'm beginning to think it's about time you retired.
SHERWOOD:	(*Thoughtfully*) Twenty thousand for the pendant and … (*Suddenly*) Er … what was that, Inspector?
HUDSON:	(*Still amused*) I said … I'm beginning to think it's about time you retired …
SHERWOOD:	You know, George … That's quite an idea! Quite an idea …

And ANTHONY SHERWOOD laughs.

THE END

Send For Francis Durbridge
When a new serial is required for "steam radio" or tv the chances are that this man from Birmingham will provide a winner by **Hal Langham**

On your home screen you are probably seeing tv's newest Durbridge serial *The Teckman Biography*. It is a story of character and suspense – the sort of story that quietly buttonholes you and keeps you waiting for more.

That's the trick of the man who wrote it – Francis Durbridge. The name is familiar? It ought to be, for it has been announced on the air countless times in the last fifteen years, generally attached to a Paul Temple radio serial.

Francis Durbridge has created in Paul Temple a character who has been passed into the language. Seven actors have portrayed him on the air. He has been seen in films, books, and newspaper strips.

"We have just finished recording the fourteen Temple series called *Paul Temple and the Gilbert Case*," Francis Durbridge told me the other day. "It will start on the Light Programme in March."

In talking about his characters in his stories you notice that Durbridge always uses the word we. We writers are fonder of the word I. But Francis Durbridge is the complete professional. He goes to the studios for rehearsals, he is in on the details of the production, and in the choice of casts.

He is a quiet man of forty-one, who has managed to stay in the shadow of Paul Temple and his wife Steve, an ageless and attractive pair whom the radio years never seem to wither.

Durbridge is a keen-faced, balding man, who looks and talks like anyone but a writer of detective stories and thrillers. Though he follows in the footsteps of Edgar Wallace, that master of thrills and output, he has no "gimmicks" like

143

Edgar's famed long cigarette-holders. Francis doesn't smoke, anyway.

He cannot admit to any hobby, doesn't play golf or do gardening, and lives in a house in Walton-on-Thames. Most mornings at nine o'clock he is in his work room-study, and he does his eight-hour shift there.

Paul Temple stories, in fact, are an industry with a big export trade. They have been broadcast and published in Sweden, Finland, Italy, Germany, Denmark, Norway, Holland, Canada, Australia and New Zealand. Francis Durbridge is quite proud of that record.

All this began in Birmingham sixteen years ago, when the young Durbridge had left Birmingham University and was setting out to be a writer. His very first performed play he did at the age of fifteen, a thriller called *The Great Dutton*, presented to family and friends in aid of charity.

In his university days, too, he had written material for the students' annual reviews, and actually performed in one. In the audience that night was a BBC Midland producer named Martyn C. Webster.

"Years later Martyn and I were associated closely in putting on Paul Temple," Durbridge recalls with a grin. "I asked him what he thought of me as an actor. 'The worst actor I ever saw,' said Martyn."

Martyn Webster and Francis Durbridge first met over the production of a serious play called *Promotion*, which was Durbridge's first radio effort. It was a success, put out from the BBC Birmingham studios, and got three repeats. Webster asked for another play, and Durbridge obliged with another winner called *Dolmans*.

"But all the time I had this idea for a radio series based on a detective character," Durbridge says. Series and serials were rare in pre-war radio.

"How did I get the name Paul Temple? I don't know. I remember I wrote down dozens of names, using telephone directories and so on, and then Paul Temple flashed into my mind. It seemed the right sort of name for the man I had in mind. My leading girl I called Louise Harvey. She was a girl reporter on a newspaper, and she wrote under the name Steve Trent. It wasn't long before the name Steve stuck to her for everything, and Steve she is."

One listener named his daughter Steve because he was so beguiled by the character as created on the air by Marjorie Westbury.

The first thriller serial by the Durbridge-Webster team was *Send For Paul Temple*. It was only a regional affair at first from Birmingham, with a Saturday morning repeat on London Regional. At the end of the run it was a national smash hit, and the BBC began to receive the sort of fan mail that they thought only happened to American soap operas.

That was in the script in 1938. There has been roughly one Paul Temple adventure every year since then. Durbridge is the top success story of British radio, one of the very small group who have made money by writing for the BBC.

He is unnerved by all this, likes to live quietly with his wife who has nothing to do with his work, except that she listens regularly to the Temple stories and watches the tv serials, and his two sons Stephen, aged twelve, and Nicholas, aged five. You see, Durbridge couldn't resist naming his son Steve!

The boys think it is rather fun to have a writer in the house and are keen, critical fans. Now television has acted on the motto Send for Paul Temple. I doubt they will capture Paul Temple from sound.

Printed in Great Britain
by Amazon

10938347R00092